An Unexpected Lady

Lelia M. Silver

Silver Summer Publishing

An Unexpected Lady

Published by Silver Summer Publishing
http://www.leliamsilver.com

The characters and events portrayed in this book are fictitious or are used fictitiously. Any similarity to real persons, living or dead, is purely coincidental and not intended by the author.

ISBN-13: 978-1-965406-01-4

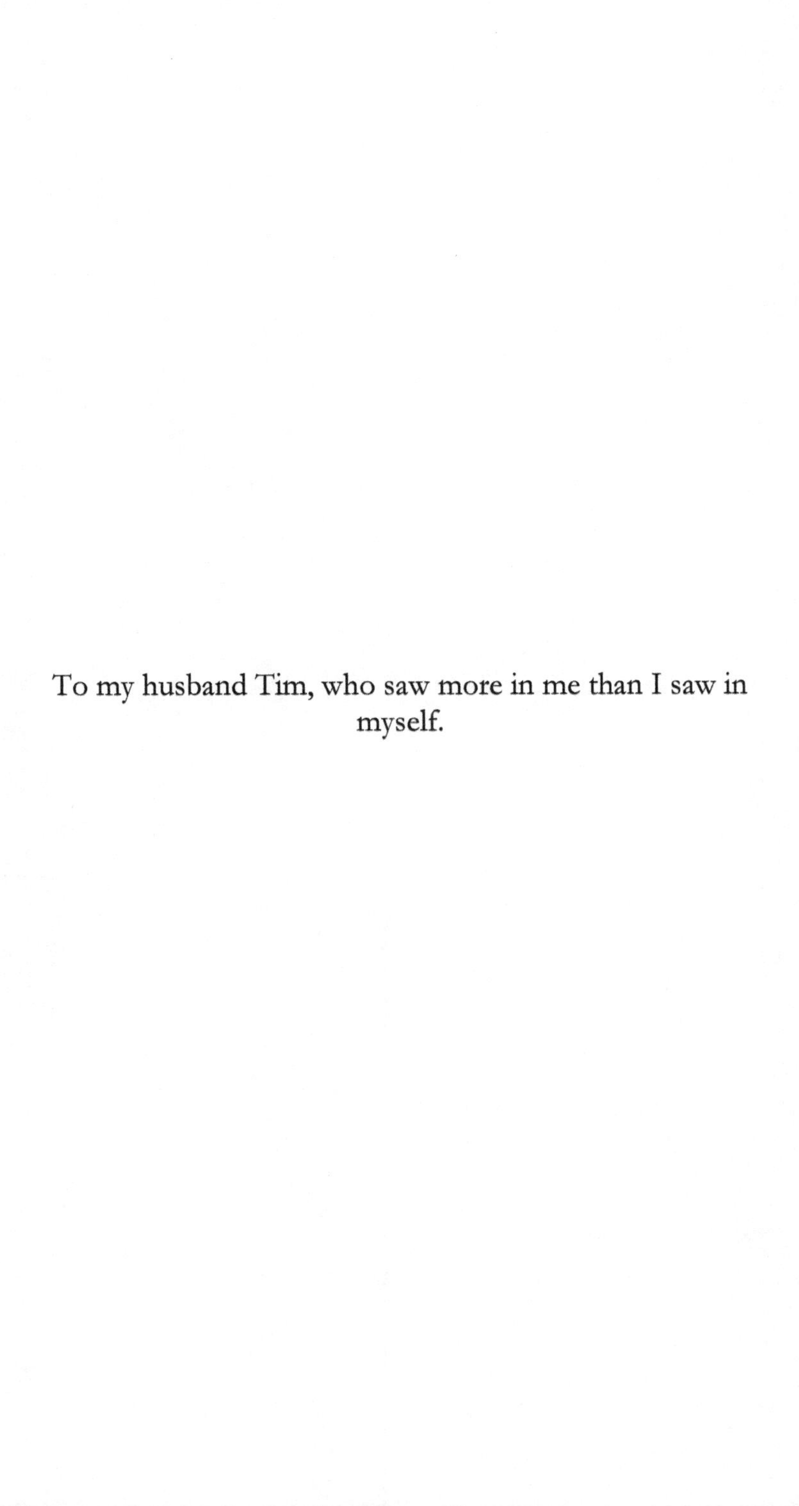

To my husband Tim, who saw more in me than I saw in myself.

ACKNOWLEDGMENTS

This book would never have gotten this far without the support and encouragement of my husband and my dear friends and family members. My thanks also go out to all those who have taken a chance and read my works. Your support and encouraging words are more appreciated than you can know. In addition, I must acknowledge the brilliance of Jane Austen. Her characters, plots, and settings are unparalleled. Of course, any mistakes are my own.

Kitty, to her very material advantage, spent the chief of her time with her two elder sisters. In society so superior to what she had generally known, her improvement was great. She was not of so ungovernable a temper as Lydia; and, removed from the influence of Lydia's example, she became, by proper attention and management, less irritable, less ignorant, and less insipid. From the further disadvantage of Lydia's society she was of course carefully kept; and though Mrs. Wickham frequently invited her to come and stay with her, with the promise of balls and young men, her father would never consent to her going.
– Pride and Prejudice

CHAPTER ONE

What an inauspicious beginning, Kitty Bennet mused as blood-curdling wails rent the air of the humble parsonage in Kent. Young William Collins had not ceased crying since the moment he had come into the world. Now, two weeks later, poor Charlotte looked positively bedraggled, and the rest of them were hardly faring any better. The only one who seemed at all well-rested was Mr. Collins, which Kitty suspected was in large part due to his ability to escape the parsonage under the guise of attending to church duties. More than once, she had been sent to fetch Mr. Collins from the church, only to find him asleep on a pew. If she had known what awaited her, she would have been sorely tempted to refuse Charlotte's request that she attend her during her confinement.

She gazed longingly out the window at the inviting gardens and warm spring sunshine. Two years ago, she would not have hesitated to abandon Charlotte for the fun of the outdoors. But time spent in her sisters' good company, without Lydia's bad influence, had changed her. She felt the weight of responsibility all too clearly now of the role she had assumed by agreeing to attend Charlotte.

A sudden silence caused hope to flutter briefly in her breast. *Silence, blessed silence!* Kitty never thought to be so grateful for the hush. Her temples throbbed from the constant caterwauling, and lack of sleep had only amplified her headache. The pins that held her mass of curls in a neat chignon were like needles jabbing her scalp.

From above stairs, the wailing started up again. She flinched at the obnoxious sound. She could stand the pressure on her head no more. She tore the pins from her hair, allowing it to cascade around her shoulders. The relief was instant, and she hurried upstairs to put the pins away on her dressing table and find the nurse.

She found the haggard woman in the nursery, cradling the child against her and bouncing him as she paced by the windows.

"Let me take him," she offered. "Wrap him up well and I will take him out to the gardens. The spring air and sunshine will be good for him."

The grateful woman hastened to do as she asked. Within ten minutes, Kitty found herself in her own spencer, cradling the baby as she walked the garden path. Her bonnet lay rejected inside in deference to the pounding headache that still held her captive.

The combination of the fresh air and warmth from the sun's rays seemed to work a miracle on the little boy. Fifteen minutes of walking had calmed him and very nearly put him to sleep. His little body had relaxed into hers and Kitty was murmuring soft nonsense to him when a commotion up the drive drew her attention. Two riders were approaching the parsonage.

She changed her direction to meet them at the gate, not wanting the visitors to disrupt the household while they were finally enjoying a well-deserved respite.

As they drew nearer, Kitty recognized Colonel Fitzwilliam, but the identity of the second rider continued to elude her. He wore his hat low over his face, preventing her from getting a good look at his features.

"Good morning!" Colonel Fitzwilliam called out, drawing his mount close to the garden gate. He dismounted to approach her, throwing the reins of his mount to his companion to hold.

"I trust your morning has been pleasant, Miss Bennet," he said agreeably.

She acquiesced, holding her voice to low tones in order to prevent waking the babe. She wondered that he did not introduce his friend; but there were many in the Fitzwilliams' circle of friends that would consider her beneath their notice.

"I have come with instructions to invite the household to dinner. My wife and her mother desire the company of your party this evening."

"I shall inform Mr. Collins, sir." Normally outgoing, Kitty dreaded the idea of being in company that evening. But the obsequious Mr. Collins would never refuse an invitation from his beloved patroness. She would be obliged to attend.

"Very good then."

His companion's horse whinnied loudly as Colonel Fitzwilliam's mount strayed too close to it.

Kitty's startled gaze rose to meet the stranger's blue eyes as he studied her intently from under the brim of his hat.

For one long moment, Kitty could not look away from him, lost in the intensity of his gaze. Then young William let out an earsplitting wail of complaint at being woken so rudely. Immediately, her attention shifted to the baby she held, and the Colonel bid her a hasty adieu, mounting his horse and trotting rapidly down the lane.

The stranger watched her unnoticed as she headed back down the path towards the house, cooing to the baby and bouncing him, before turning his mount to follow his friend.

*****

Nathaniel Watson was not a man who tolerated idiocy. He ground his teeth in an effort to control himself as Lady Catherine began another of her long-winded discourses. When he had accepted Colonel Fitzwilliam's offer to visit him and his new bride, he had not expected to have the mother-in-law in constant attendance also. One would think the woman would accept that her rightful place was in the dower house!

The occupants of the drawing room seemed to accept her presence as matter-of-course. He desperately needed a distraction, but their dinner guests were not expected to arrive for half an hour yet. In an attempt to assuage his temper, he allowed his mind to wander to the expected guests.

He had jumped at the chance to accompany Fitzwilliam to the parsonage in order to extend the invitation. The fresh air had whisked away the vestiges of the dank drawing room and invigorated him. Even his high-spirited mount seemed pleased to have escaped the confines of his stall, surging and shying at any movement, eager for a good run.

They had approached the gates of the parsonage all too soon. Enthralled with the joy of the ride, he did not notice the woman who came to meet them until they were practically upon her. She studied him curiously as he took Fitzwilliam's reins, but appeared to dismiss his presence as his companion began to speak.

He had frowned as he studied her. Her dress marked her as genteel, but her hair was loose, cascading around her shoulders in lush, satin waves. She did not wear a bonnet, in utter disregard for the bounds of propriety. And she did not even appear embarrassed to be caught so!

Still, something about her intrigued him. Her features were dainty and feminine, pretty- but nothing extraordinary. A small part of him admired her audacity to appear so carefree in public, and he could not deny that he found her attractive with her tresses flowing free. Still, there was nothing at all about her that would set her apart from the masses of debutantes seeking a title and a fortune.

In his distraction, he had neglected to pay attention to his high-strung mount. Colonel Fitzwilliam's gentle roan ambled too close to his own gelding, and his mount struck out at the other horse, whinnying loudly in protest.

The young woman's eyes had snapped up at the interruption. Instantly, he was drowning in her clear, bottle green gaze. Her eyes held a hint of irritation, but any other discoveries he might have made were lost when a baby's cry split the air. His eyes had been drawn downward to a bundle she had been cradling that he had hitherto ignored.

He had been startled to realize the bundle she held was actually a child. What was she doing with a baby? She certainly did not seem to be old enough for the child to be hers.

Colonel Fitzwilliam had come scurrying back to collect his mount as the cries grew in intensity. Nathaniel had watched the woman as she hurried away. He still could not explain why the idea of the child being hers bothered him so much.

He noted with pleasure that the time had neared for their guests to arrive. Surely now some of his questions would be answered.

As if on cue, the door opened to admit their guests.

"A Mr. William Collins, Miss Maria Lucas, and Miss Catherine Bennet," the footman intoned drolly.

Nathaniel studied the additions to their party as introductions were made. He was inexplicably disappointed to see that the young lady he had admired earlier had been restored to her proper dress. She wore a simple, yet elegant, gown and her hair was curled and piled on top of her head in the latest fashion. He saw none of the free spirit that had so enthralled him earlier. In their place was a dull, subdued girl that he easily dismissed as unimportant.

*****

Kitty barely paid any heed as the introductions were made. Her mother would have been horrified to note with what little enthusiasm she shared the room with the decidedly single Marquess of Rockingham. Her head pounded fiercely from the myriads of pins that pressed against her scalp, holding up her mass of hair. In her exhaustion, every movement was excruciating, and when she moved it felt as if her limbs were weighted down with stones.

She took a seat next to Maria Lucas on the settee and tried to maintain an attentive air as Mr. Collins greeted his patroness with excessive admiration. Lady Catherine monopolized the conversation, her sharp, intrusive voice pausing only for Mr. Collins' flattery.

It was with some relief that the entire party went in to dine. Kitty found herself seated, in a surprising move, to Lady Catherine's left, with the Marquess seated across from her and Mr. Collins to her left. She tried not to allow the shock to show on her face as she took her seat.

It soon appeared that Lady Catherine had engineered such a situation for a purpose. As sister of the despised Elizabeth Darcy, who had upset her long hoped for plans, Lady Catherine was intent on exposing all her deficiencies for the table at large.

"How is your sister, Miss Bennet?" Lady Catherine asked with a smirk. "I hope she is not finding the rigors of Town too challenging."

"You will have to be more specific as to which sister you are referring to," Kitty replied. "I have four, as you are aware, two of which are in Town at the moment."

Lady Catherine sniffed irritably. "I was referring to Miss Elizabeth. She is the only one of your sisters I am acquainted personally with, although I am aware of your youngest sister and that patched-up marriage of hers."

Kitty blushed at the insinuation, but ignored the jab and responded mildly, "My sister Elizabeth is enjoying the opportunity to sample the pleasures of Town. There is a stubbornness about her that never can bear to be frightened at the will of others. Her courage rises with every attempt to intimidate her. The trait has only grown since she has become Mrs. Darcy."

Lady Catherine frowned at the mention of Elizabeth's married name. "She always did give her opinion very decidedly for so young a person. I am sure my nephew will tire of that soon enough. He will turn to those befitting his station before long."

Kitty lifted her chin. "You will have to excuse me for choosing to believe otherwise. It would hardly encourage sisterly affection if I did not wish the best for my sister in her marriage."

The lady harrumphed and momentarily applied herself to her meal, allowing Kitty to sigh in relief and attend to her own plate. But the reprieve was only momentary, and soon Lady Catherine was on the attack again.

"I hope that you have applied yourself to becoming accomplished in the areas which your sister neglected. No excellence in music, or any other pursuit, is to be acquired without constant practice. I have told *Miss Bennet* this several times; she will never play really well unless she practices more."

Kitty raised a brow at Lady Catherine's use of her sister's maiden name. "I believe Mr. Darcy finds Mrs. Darcy's playing to be quite satisfactory. Exquisite even. I fear I cannot say the same about my own. My sister Mary is said to be quite accomplished at the pianoforte, but I never showed any affinity for the instrument."

"Do you draw then?"

"Not at all."

"I never heard of such a thing!" She turned and applied to the Marquess for the first time in the conversation. "Lord Rockingham, surely you have never heard of such a deficiency in a young lady's education among your circles."

He met Kitty's eyes over the table, his expression indecipherable. "No. I have not."

Kitty lowered her eyes to her plate. She was beginning to tire of this line of inquiry. An attack on her person was not what she had had in mind for the evening's entertainment, especially in her current state. She had endeavored to address Lady Catherine with every appearance of civility, even when that lady had not shown her the same consideration.

Fortunately, Lady Catherine believed her point to be made from Lord Rockingham's reply and left off interrogating Kitty in favor of expounding upon her own many virtues. Mr. Collins was eager to support her in this line of discussion and he inserted his own praises on the subject with delighted alacrity.

Kitty could not help but feel her own inferiority at that moment, and lacking the courage that her sister possessed, applied herself to her dinner without an upward glance.

*****

Nathaniel looked forward to the separating of the sexes after dinner with some trepidation. Had Colonel Fitzwilliam been the only other gentleman present, he would have looked to the occasion with pleasure, but the presence of the parson complicated matters. He had the uneasy feeling that he would become the focus of the man's obsequious manners in Lady Catherine's absence.

He was right to be so concerned, for upon the ladies' removal to the drawing room, Mr. Collins shifted his attention to his prestigious person with such flattery and groveling that Nathaniel began to suspect that the parson had put much forethought into arranging his elegant compliments. Colonel Fitzwilliam watched it all with a glint of laughter in his eye.

At length, Nathaniel could stand it no longer, and his suggestion that they join the ladies in the drawing room was met with approval.

They entered the room to find Lady Catherine holding court over the ladies. There was nothing beneath that lady's attention when it could furnish her with an occasion of dictating to others. He noted that Miss Bennet was again the object of Lady Catherine's attention and he could not help but pity the young woman her fate.

He purposefully took a seat as far away from the great lady as possible. Colonel Fitzwilliam joined him on the outskirts of the group, while Mr. Collins eagerly sought out a seat beside his patroness in order to further ingratiate himself.

The two gentlemen began to speak in low tones as Lady Catherine lectured.

"Well, Fitzwilliam, how has marriage been treating you? I do not envy you your new relations."

"Ah, but you forget that they are not new. I have been attending my aunt for many years now." He smiled indulgently at the thought of his new bride. "I find I am quite enjoying married life. Anne is very accommodating and she makes very few demands on my time. We are content to be in each other's company."

"You claim to feel some affection for her, yet you allow her mother to usurp her rightful place in the household. I confess that I am confused by your actions."

"Anne has no desire for confrontation. My father has offered us the use of one of his estates in the North. We will withdraw there shortly, allowing Lady Catherine to live out her days at Rosings. She could not be happy without some employment to occupy her. Here, she can be most active among the cottagers, sallying forth to settle their differences, silence their complaints, and scold them into harmony and plenty. Our absence will hardly be noted. But *hers* will be most appreciated in our new home."

Here, Kitty was dispatched across the room to display her limited skills at the pianoforte for the company. Nathaniel suspected it was an attempt on Lady Catherine's part to embarrass the young woman further, for she had specifically noted over dinner that she had no affinity for the instrument.

As she began to hesitantly pick out a simple tune, Colonel Fitzwilliam said slyly, "Are you still as confirmed a bachelor as ever? I thought perhaps some young lady had caught your eye earlier. Miss Bennet is thought to be uncommonly pretty."

Nathaniel turned his head to lazily observe her at the instrument before declaring, "Yes, but so are half the daughters of the Ton. There is nothing extraordinary enough about her to tempt me."

Kitty faltered at that moment in her playing, her color high, and he thought for a moment that she had overheard their conversation. But he soon dismissed the notion, in favor of the thought that her concentration would by necessity have been fully upon the instrument and not upon themselves. The blush upon her cheeks was easily explained away as embarrassment over the faulty notes.

He gave no more thought to the matter, instead turning the discussion to more agreeable topics.

*****

It was indeed embarrassment that brought color to Kitty's cheeks, but it was not due to her faulty playing. She knew herself to be unequal to the task of performing, and so had no false hopes that she would be able to complete her tenure at the instrument without mistakes.

Her blush was due to the comments of a certain gentleman, which although not loud enough to carry to those gathered on the other side of the room, were quite loud enough to be overheard by her.

Kitty parted from the company that night feeling very small indeed. She had known herself to lack the wit and vivacity of Elizabeth and to be inferior in beauty to Jane. She had not the knowledge of Mary, neither her ability to play and sing, nor did she possess Lydia's high spirits. But it was the first time she had ever felt herself to be positively *ordinary*. She had nothing to recommend her beyond her newly acquired family connections from sisters' recent marriages.

She wished at that moment for the comfort of her sisters' arms. She remembered many a time in their youth when they had crowded five to a bed when one or the other of them had suffered some slight or set-back. How she longed for someone to confide in, to ease her wounded spirit!

But she had only a pillow to entrust her tears to, and an empty room to hear her sorrows.

CHAPTER TWO

The next morning dawned bright and cheerful, and with it it brought a desire to escape that dreadful house. For the moment, young William Collins slept on, and Kitty felt justified in setting off for a short walk in the park in order to sort her feelings from the night before.

Her headache from the day prior had subsided enough that she was comfortable wearing her bonnet, even with her hair in a simple up-do.

She set off down one of the less traveled lanes of the park, hoping for some privacy. It was not to be. She had only traversed a short distance when a rider approached her from behind. She moved to the side of the lane to allow the rider to pass.

Instead, the clip-clop of the horse's hooves slowed and drew abreast of her. Curious and a little confused, she turned to observe her companion as he reined in beside her.

Her attention was so immediately caught by the superior example of horseflesh before her that she neglected to detect the identity of its rider. A chuckle from above finally drew her attention.

"I am glad to see that Abaccus has met with your approval, Miss Bennet," Nathaniel said with a warm smile.

"He moves beautifully," she agreed, casting her eye once more over the tall bay.

"Yes, he has a very smooth gait. A touch too high-spirited, but I would not have a mount any other way."

"He must be great fun to ride," Kitty said enviously.

He tilted his head curiously to study her, recognizing the jealous tone in her voice. "Do you enjoy riding, Miss Bennet?"

"I do," she admitted. "But I do not often have the opportunity. The horses on my father's estate are mostly for use around the farm."

He raised an eyebrow sardonically. "A farm horse is a very different animal than a Thoroughbred like Abaccus. I think you would find him to be more than you can handle."

She frowned at his condescending manner and replied, "I am sure many would agree with you. If you will excuse me now, I would like to continue my walk." She turned and resumed walking.

Nathaniel scowled at her retreating form and swung out of the saddle to follow. He easily caught up to her in a few long strides.

"May I join you?" he asked.

Her bonnet hid her glower. "If you would like," she said politely, her voice cool. She picked up the pace, which he easily matched.

"Have I said something to offend you, Miss Bennet?" he asked at the decidedly frosty silence that stretched between them.

"Whatever would give you that idea?" she replied sarcastically.

Nathaniel was taken aback. His mouth hung open for a moment before he snapped it shut, stunned into silence. In all his twenty-seven years, no woman had ever spoken to him so!

He had encountered simpering misses, who agreed with every word that came out of his mouth, and accomplished flirts who enticed and teased with every utterance. But no woman had ever treated him with such disregard. If he did not know better, he would think that she did not wish for the privilege of his company!

He puzzled over how to respond to her comment. "Miss Bennet, if you truly do not wish for my company, I assure you that you may say so freely."

She turned her head to look at him, still walking furiously. "I– " Her foot caught on a root in that instant and she went stumbling forward.

There was no time for thought, only for action. Nathaniel, every bit the gentleman he had been raised to be, immediately stepped before her to prevent her from tumbling to the ground.

She fell into his arms with a cry. He grunted as her full weight hit his chest and closed his arms around her to steady her.

"Are you all right, Miss Bennet?" he asked solicitously.

She raised her head to meet his eyes, her cheeks flushed with embarrassment. "I believe so, Lord Rockingham. I am dreadfully sorry."

With the immediate danger past, Nathaniel could not help but notice how delicate her petite frame felt in his arms. Her eyes were a deeper shade of green today, he realized, and in their depths he could see chagrin and a lingering trace of hurt. He wondered at that hurt and was opening his mouth to speak when a cry from down the lane drew both of their attentions.

"MISS BENNET!" Mr. Collins stood at the end of the lane, where it intersected with the main path, his mouth agape.

Nathaniel was suddenly aware that he still held Miss Bennet in his arms, most inappropriately. He released her immediately, a sinking feeling in his gut appearing as he realized how their stance would have looked to the parson.

Kitty hurriedly took several steps away from Lord Rockingham, confused by the sudden bereavement she felt as Nathaniel let her go.

Mr. Collins advanced down the lane toward them, his short legs carrying him as fast as they would go. Despite the gravity of the moment, the absurdity of his movements elicited a strangled giggle from Kitty. Nathaniel turned to look down at her dancing eyes and could not help but grin in return.

He sobered quickly as the diminutive man stopped in front of Miss Bennet and drew himself up to his full height. "I am ashamed, Miss Bennet, to call you my cousin! I had thought you to be an upright woman, bound by propriety. But I find instead that I have been harboring a harlot!"

Kitty gasped at the strong words, and Nathaniel felt his own ire rising at the pompous fool.

Mr. Collins continued, "You are no better than that scandalous sister of yours, trying to seduce a member of the Quality! You will return to the house at once and pack your belongings! I will not have a temptress in my household, influencing my wife and child! When I complete my business with Lady Catherine, I will expect you to be ready to depart for the stagecoach immediately!"

Nathaniel watched in horror as the young woman bowed her head and hurried off in the direction of the parsonage, her cheeks burning with embarrassment and rage at the undeserved disparagement.

Nathaniel braced himself for a similar barrage to be heaped upon him as Mr. Collins shifted his focus to him. Instead, he stood in shock as the man proceeded to heap apologies upon him for Miss Bennet's supposed advances. He was repeatedly assured that the young woman would be dealt with properly and that there would be no damage to his own reputation.

His mouth settled in a grim line as he listened to the man. Was Miss Bennet to hold all the blame for the compromising encounter, with no opportunity for explanation? And was he to be completely absolved of all responsibility, simply because of his status as a peer of the realm?

The discrepancy was too great, even for his privileged mind. Troubled, he cut off Mr. Collins. "I have some matters of business to attend to, Mr. Collins, and I believe you have a meeting with Lady Catherine. I recommend that you appear punctually, as that great lady does not like to be kept waiting. Please excuse me."

He turned his back and walked away, leaving the little man to bluster and sputter his compliments incoherently. He had some matters to discuss with Colonel Fitzwilliam.

*****

Kitty's cheeks burned with embarrassment and righteous indignation as she began the process of packing her trunk. Charlotte had offered her the help of one of the maids, but she preferred to complete the task herself.

Insufferable man! The audacity! To accuse her of such filthy things, without even asking for an explanation when he stumbled upon them! It was not as if they had done anything wrong. She had stumbled, and Lord Rockingham had caught her. There was nothing improper in that. It was all a simple misunderstanding.

But she knew that in Mr. Collins' eyes, she was already ruined. It mattered not what the real story was. He had jumped to conclusions and condemned her. The tale would spread. Mr. Collins was incapable of keeping any tidbit of gossip to himself. Lady Catherine was undoubtedly already aware of her disgrace.

That lady would do her best to spread the gossip, to ensure her humiliation in all the best society. Her hatred for Lizzy had already shown itself to extend to her relations. She was to be sent home in shame.

As for Lord Rockingham- she banged the lid of the trunk down angrily- that man would suffer no ills from the occasion. Only *her* reputation would be damaged. Compromised, that was what she was now. Damaged goods. No one would want her.

She knew him better than to think he would offer for her. He was too far above her. Why should he- a *Marquess*- align himself with her, a little nobody from Hertfordshire?

She sat down heavily on the trunk and wept bitterly for what might have been.

CHAPTER THREE

Nathaniel sought out his friend, Colonel Fitzwilliam, upon his return to Rosings. The older man was sequestered in his personal sitting room with his wife. Nathaniel felt all the awkwardness of intruding upon their privacy upon entering the room and finding them settled by the fire, she with some mending upon her lap, and he with a book in his hand.

"Forgive me for intruding upon you," he apologized with a bow. "I did not expect to come upon you so agreeably engaged."

Anne graced him with a gentle smile. "You need not apologize, Lord Rockingham. I know my husband enjoys your company. And I have long desired to know such a good friend of Richard's better. Please, sit."

He joined them by the fireplace, perching at the edge of his seat and fiddling with the brim of his hat. He proceeded with all the expected niceties, unsure of how to approach his topic with the lady's unexpected company. For some length of time he continued on in this manner, until finally, Colonel Fitzwilliam stopped him with a knowing smile.

"What did you really come to talk to me about, Nathaniel? You may speak freely in front of Anne. She will not repeat anything you say."

Nathaniel sighed. "I am afraid it is a matter of some delicacy." He got up to pace. "This morning, while out riding, as is my custom, I stumbled upon Miss Bennet taking her morning constitutional. She admired my mount; I asked to accompany her on her walk. A short time later, she tripped over a root, and I caught her in order to prevent a fall."

He turned to face Colonel Fitzwilliam with some regret and trepidation. "Mr. Collins stumbled upon us at that exact moment and witnessed what he believed to be a tender embrace."

He resumed his pacing. "There was no opportunity to correct his misapprehension. He immediately began to attack Miss Bennet, insinuating- well, I shall not repeat it in front of a lady. Let us just say that he was not complimentary. In short order, he dispatched her to pack her bags and return to her home. I naturally assumed that I would be his next victim, but such was not the case. He was all apologies, telling me that the girl would be punished appropriately for trying to seduce me!"

Colonel Fitzwilliam shared a look with his wife and responded mildly, "It sounds like you are in a bit of a predicament."

Nathaniel came back to collapse in his chair, running a hand through his hair. "Yes. I find his allegations toward Miss Bennet to be repulsive, and I cannot consciously allow him to go on thinking her a fallen woman."

Anne put down her needlework and looked him straight in the eye. Her voice was low and her tone serious as she said, "It is too late for apologies and explanations, Lord Rockingham. If I know my mother and her parson (as I understand, he was in to see her already this morning), word of this incident will spread ferociously. My mother has held a deep-seated hatred for the Miss Bennets ever since their older sister, Miss Elizabeth Bennet, married my cousin, Mr. Darcy. She had intended him for me, you see. My mother will do all in that is in her power to ruin Miss Catherine Bennet in the eyes of society."

Nathaniel frowned at this announcement. "But what am I to do about it?"

"You know already what you must do, Lord Rockingham," Anne said calmly. "Are you looking to us to absolve your responsibility toward her?"

He frowned at the insinuation and drew himself up. "I assure you I have no such intention."

"Then your actions are clear. You have compromised her. You must marry her. It is the only honorable thing to do."

He rose at her words to stand by the window, staring out at the gardens below as his mind pondered this development. Husband and wife waited patiently for his response.

Finally, he turned back to them. "You are correct. It is the only right and honorable thing to do."

Fitzwilliam smiled broadly. "It appears you are not such a confirmed bachelor as I thought you were, Nathaniel. I look forward to the wedding. I do hope we will be invited."

Nathaniel shot his friend a disgruntled look as Anne spoke up, "I believe you must have some letters to write, now that you are resolved upon your course of action. Your mother, I believe, would be most interested."

Nathaniel bowed and dismissed himself. "You are right, of course. Excuse me."

*****

Nathaniel seated himself at his writing desk, a freshly mended pen in hand and a crisp sheet of stationery before him. He had not an inkling of how he should begin to inform his mother of such news.

She would be disappointed that he had allowed himself to be caught in such a predicament, as unintentional as it had been. She had raised him to comport himself better than that. She would be proud though, to know that he was doing the right thing by declaring himself. She might even be pleased at the thought of a daughter-in-law. Although she had never pressured him to marry and have a family, he knew she desired grandchildren.

With these thoughts to buoy him, he set his pen to paper.
'My dearest Mother,

I write to inform you of events that have recently transpired that I hope will have a pleasant outcome upon both of our lives. I have lately become acquainted with a lovely young lady here in Kent. She is of humble connections. I believe her father is a gentleman farmer, but she has two sisters recently married to two quite well-known and respected gentleman; namely, Mr. Charles Bingley of Chetborn and Mr. Fitzwilliam Darcy of Pemberley. I believe you are aware of them, probably more so than I am. I came upon her this morning as she was walking and joined her for a stroll. As we traversed, she tripped and would have fallen, except by some chance I managed to catch her. While we were thus occupied, the local parson, a small-minded man with few scruples, stumbled upon us. I cannot repeat the accusations laid upon Miss Bennet from that door. Suffice to say that I was shocked and appalled by his manner of addressing her. Myself, he treated with considerably less acrimony. I thought little more on the subject, until it was brought to my attention that news of this encounter would be spread and endanger the young lady's reputation. I resolved then that I must take some action. I intend to make her my bride. It is with some shame that I write these words, having always hoped to enter the matrimonial state without scandal. I know you will be disappointed by my actions, but I intend to do all I can to make up for the young lady's lost opportunities. I accept full responsibility for my actions. I can but hope that the prospect of a felicitous daughter will soften your disillusionment with me. I travel tomorrow to seek her hand, as the young lady has already been sent off in disgrace by her obnoxious cousin, the parson. Forgive me. I remain your humble son,

Nathaniel Watson"

He concluded the letter with some satisfaction that he had conveyed the facts with dignity, and then addressed and sealed it. He placed it on the tray to be sent out with the morning's correspondence. With the necessary matters seen to, he was free to examine his own emotions on the subject.

They were decidedly conflicted. It had all happened so quickly. One innocuous gesture and his world was tossed on its head. All that he had known and carefully controlled was gone, and now he was faced with a new reality, one that involved a wife. So many changes would have to be made. The dower house would have to be made ready for his mother. The mistress' apartments adjoining his own would have to be prepared. The servants would need to be told.

But before all that could happen, he had to apply for and be granted her hand in marriage. He would have to travel on the morrow.

The realization dawned on him that he had no idea where Miss Bennet was from, and therefore, where she had been sent back to. He set his mouth in a grim line. There was much to be accomplished before his journey.

He rose to begin the preparations, starting with asking Fitzwilliam just where Miss Bennet lived.

*****

Nathaniel reined in Abaccus at the lane leading up to Longbourn, the home of Miss Catherine Bennet. The prospect that lay before him was unimpressive but charming, in its own way.

The sun reflected off the modest brick home, casting it in a warm glow. Geese, ducks, and chickens flocked in the yard. The lane was lined with trees and in the distance he could make out a pretty little grove that he imagined would make a pleasant retreat on a summer's afternoon.

It was very different than his own sprawling home, but he found it reflected favorably on the young lady that inhabited it. He shook his head in amazement. To have raised five daughters in that small home! It must have been chaos. It was no wonder that Miss Bennet allowed herself to be disregarded so easily.

He nudged his mount forward.

As he drew up to the entrance, a manservant came to greet him and take his horse. He was directed inside, where the housekeeper, a Mrs. Hill, took his overcoat and gloves and informed him that Mr. Bennet could be found in his study, as usual.

Nathaniel wondered at the qualifier, "as usual," but had no time to question it as Kitty stepped into the hall at that moment to find out what all the bustle was about.

"Hill, whatever..." Her voice trailed off at the sight of him, and she froze in shock. Her eyes widened in surprise. "Lord Rockingham."

He bowed mockingly. "Miss Bennet."

She flushed at his tone and raised her chin defiantly. "We were not expecting visitors today, my Lord."

"I gathered as much. I have come to speak to your father, Miss Bennet. Mrs. Hill was just about to show me in. If you will excuse me." He stepped past her and followed the housekeeper, leaving Kitty standing in the hall staring after them, confusion evident upon her face.

*****

Nathaniel was mildly surprised at the first fluttering of nerves in his stomach as he stood outside Mr. Bennet's study door. There was no reason he should not expect his request to be granted. Any father would have to be insane to turn down an offer from the Marquess of Rockingham. Especially the father of a girl who had been compromised, who in all likelihood would never entertain another offer, at least not any one near as good as his.

"Mr. Bennet?" Mrs. Hill knocked on the door. "You have a visitor here to see you."

He heard a male voice from within. "Send him in, please."He took a deep breath to calm his nerves and went in.

*****

Kitty paced the drawing room, wringing her hands, while Mary pounded away at the pianoforte in the corner. Whatever could Lord Rockingham want with her father? Had he come to correct the sensationalized reports of their embrace and excuse himself for damaging her reputation? She dismissed immediately the idea that he could have come to offer for her. He had made it abundantly clear that she was beneath his notice.

Thank goodness her mother was in town visiting with her Aunt Phillips! She flinched as she recalled her mother's flustered attentions to Mr. Darcy upon his engagement to Lizzy. The Marquess was superior to even that great man. She could only imagine how her mother would react to his presence.

Kitty worried her bottom lip and turned to the window, seeking a distraction for her troubled mind. The gardens below beckoned to her, and she made up her mind without hesitation. She fetched her bonnet and pelisse and hurried outside. Whatever business Lord Rockingham had with her father, there could be nothing further he had to say to *her*.

*****

Meanwhile, Nathaniel found himself closeted with Mr. Bennet in what was starting to become a most uncomfortable interview.

"I understand, Lord Rockingham, that you find yourself in a decidedly unfortunate predicament. Kitty would be a less than prudent match for you. I expect that you had hoped for rather more in a wife than my silly daughter. The circumstances, however, warrant it. I appreciate your coming forward to claim her hand, but I must say that it seems a little presumptuous on your part."

"Presumptuous?!" Nathaniel sputtered, affronted. "I beg your pardon, sir!"

Mr. Bennet smiled at his reaction and responded mildly, "You heard me correctly, my Lord. It seems rather hasty of you to seek my consent, when you have yet to obtain my daughter's."

Nathaniel frowned, realizing that this was the case. "I assumed the answer would be obvious. She will receive no better offer; under the circumstances it is unlikely that she will receive any more at all."

Mr. Bennet steepled his hands together and leaned back in his chair. "That may indeed be the case," he acknowledged. "But I will not force any of my daughters, no matter how silly they may be, to marry against their will. Obtain her consent, and you shall have mine."

Nathaniel scowled, but bowed to the older man's wishes. Hill was called for and applied to for Miss Kitty's whereabouts, and Nathaniel soon found himself in the garden, chasing after a rapidly disappearing bonnet.

"Miss Bennet!" he called, taking long strides in order to close the gap between them. "Please wait, Miss Bennet. I wish to speak with you."

She paused at his voice and slowly turned on her heel to face him, her eyes wary.

"You can be at no loss, Miss Bennet, to understand the reason of my journey hither."

She raised her chin defiantly. "Indeed, you are quite mistaken, my Lord. I have not been at all able to account for the honor of your visit."

He frowned. "Surely, the circumstances of your departure from Kent must give you some clue as to my presence here."

"Not at all, I assure you."

Nathaniel found this hard to believe, but pressed forward with his declaration. "I pride myself on my sincerity and frankness in difficult situations, and I shall certainly not depart from it now. Irreparable damage has been done to your reputation, and it was at least partly done by my hand. I consider myself an honorable man, and as such, there is only one course of action. I have come here today to claim your hand in marriage."

She sucked in a sharp breath and turned her head away from him, hiding her face behind the brim of her bonnet. Nathaniel found himself annoyed by the gesture, as it prevented him from reading her facial expressions, but allowed her the time she needed to process his comments.

Shielded from his intent gaze she closed her eyes. She remembered vividly Lydia's disgrace and her own part in it. Now, she was forced to relive the shame, but this time, the consequences were hers to bear. Carefully, she weighed his words. The likelihood of another offer was slim. She certainly would never entertain another one as good as the one before her. Yet, she remembered fondly her own long-held desire to marry for love. Could she really abandon that? She had seen the disparity between her older sisters' felicitous marriages and Lydia's disastrous one. What a difference love made!

Her mouth thinned. Love was not an option now. She would have to make the best of the situation she found herself in. With that firm resolve she raised her head to find his gaze still upon her.

She kept her face and voice firmly neutral. "I find my options are very limited, my Lord. I accept your offer."

Nathaniel felt a small thrill go through him upon hearing her words of affirmation, but he kept his response dispassionate. "Shall we return and inform your father then?"

She nodded reluctantly. He offered her his arm, as he expected one should their affianced. Kitty hesitated briefly before taking it and allowing him to guide her back to the house. She deposited him in the drawing room with her sister Mary and one of the maids and sought out her father in his study.

"Have you accepted him, then?"

"I have."

"He is rich, to be sure, and you may have more fine clothes and fine carriages than Jane and Lizzy together. I hope you shall be happy."

Kitty had no response to such a comment and could only suppose her father would have reacted very differently if it was Lizzy standing before him.

"Be sure to invite your betrothed to dinner. I am sure your mother will be eager to meet him. I can only imagine her joy upon realizing his possession of a title." Her father seemed to find the prospect of her mother meeting Lord Rockingham to be quite humorous, but Kitty could not see any humor in the situation.

She inclined her head and excused herself from her father's presence to return to the drawing room. She slipped back into the room to find Mary still pounding away at the pianoforte and Lord Rockingham sitting by the window, looking very bored.

She reluctantly crossed the room to take a seat near him. He looked up at her upon her arrival with something akin to relief.

"So it is settled then?" he asked.

She nodded, afraid her voice would betray her frazzled emotions if she spoke.

Nathaniel watched her with something akin to pity. It was obvious she had no more joy in the situation than he did. At least, though, he had had a choice in the matter. She had really had no further options than to accept him. Now, she found herself attached to a near perfect stranger. Their acquaintance was limited to days, and the extent of their conversations had been a diatribe by Lady Catherine and a discussion of his horse, which had ended with him offending her. It was not an auspicious beginning to their relationship.

Kitty finally gathered her courage to speak. "I am to invite you to dinner tonight. I trust you do not have any prior engagements?"

Nathaniel smiled wryly. "I do not."

"My mother will be delighted to hear that when she arrives home at Longbourn. She is visiting my Aunt Phillips in Meryton at the moment, but she takes great pride in her ability to set a fine table for any guests at a moment's notice."

Nathaniel doubted that her best table could at all compare to the finery he was used to sitting down to, but he acknowledged her statement with a nod.

"Do you plan to stay in the area for long, Lord Rockingham?" Kitty asked.

He frowned, not having given the subject much thought. "Perhaps a week or so. Long enough to have the marriage documents drafted and signed. Then I must return to London to procure a license and inform my mother."

Kitty nodded and he added slowly, "Will you travel to London yourself to procure your trousseau?"

"I imagine my mother will insist upon it, though my father will begrudge the expense. I have relatives in Grace Church Street we shall likely stay with."

"Perhaps while you are in town I can escort you round to see my mother. I am sure she will be eager to meet the new Lady Rockingham."

Kitty swallowed hard at his use of the title in connection with her. It all felt so foreign, as if he were speaking about some other, unknown, person. She only hoped she would not be an embarrassment to him.

They stiltedly discussed further trivial matters until the sound of the front door opening and her mother's voice brought Kitty to her feet. "You will have to excuse me, my Lord. I cannot allow her to hear the news from anyone but myself. I must go to her at once."

He acquiesced, not knowing how prudent her suggestion was to be. Kitty followed her mother up to her dressing room and made the important communication. Very soon, a shriek could be heard from above stairs, which caused Nathaniel quite a start, and even Mary floundered in her playing for the racket.

He rose to peer out the doorway at the stairs, wondering at his betrothed's well-being. Shortly, she appeared on the stairway, her face flushed with embarrassment upon observing his countenance in the door frame. She passed by him, murmuring as she did so, "My mother shall be down shortly to receive you, my Lord."

When said lady did appear soon after, she could hardly speak for the honor of having a peer of the realm in her parlor. Kitty rejoiced that her mother's earlier effusions were heard only by herself, even if there was still something to be wished for in her mother's behavior toward the gentleman.

Nathaniel did not have long to endure this particularly trial-some woman, as she shortly hurried off to speak to Hill about that evening's menu.

Kitty regarded Nathaniel sympathetically. He rose to pace to the window, feeling exquisitely the confines of the small room.

She took pity on the man, and offered him a reprieve. "Would you care to take a turn about the gardens, Lord Rockingham?"

He accepted eagerly, and they proceeded out of doors, with Mary to serve as chaperone following a suitable distance behind.

It was some time before they returned to the house, and when they did so, it was only to partake in the meal and the perfunctory evening entertainment. Soon afterwards, Nathaniel dismissed himself to return to the rooms he had hired at the local inn, with the promise of returning in two days time with the marriage contract.

Both parties found themselves relieved at the prospect of a short separation. He had found her relations to be taxing to his civility, although the time spent in her presence was pleasant enough.

She found herself in need of time in order to process the turn her life had taken and the new reality of what was to come.

CHAPTER FOUR

Nathaniel returned in the agreed upon two days, and left soon after with the signed contract. He proceeded on to London, where his bride-to-be was soon to join him at her Aunt and Uncle Gardiner's home in Cheapside.

Nathaniel turned Abaccus down a well-lit street in Town. He was tired from several hours in the saddle, but there was still one more matter to be dealt with before he could turn himself over to his valet and retire for the night. He could make out the light through the draperies in the front parlor as he reined in Abaccus before the well-appointed townhouse. She was waiting up for him.

He had known she would be when he had sent an express to inform her of his arrival. He was not looking forward to the interview to come. He felt like a small boy in trouble again as he climbed the steps and entered the house.

"Good evening, my Lord." The butler greeted him at the entrance, taking his overcoat and gloves. "Lady Rockingham desires you attend her in the front parlor upon your earliest convenience."

"Thank you, Smith. I shall go to her at once."

He paused before the door to take a deep breath and compose himself before he went through it.

His mother looked up with a soft smile at his entrance and came forward to greet him.

"Nathaniel! What a pleasure to see you. I had not expected you to visit so soon after your last correspondence. I do hope your journey went well?" She kissed his cheek and directed him to a seat beside hers.

He took the chair she offered. "It was uneventful."

"I am glad to hear that. Now tell me about my soon to be daughter-in-law. I assume she has accepted you." Cecelia Watson had never been a woman to beat around the bush, which was something he had always appreciated about her. There was no wondering what she was thinking or about to do. She was forthright and outspoken.

"She has, albeit reluctantly. Her name is Catherine Bennet, but her family calls her Kitty. She is the daughter of a gentleman farmer in Hertfordshire, near the village of Meryton."

His mother dismissed this information. "Yes, your letter said as much. Tell me about *her*, as a person. What is she like?"

He thought for a moment and answered slowly, "She is amiable, I suppose. I think she is very used to being forgotten about, as she is one of five sisters. On the surface, she seems to be a very ordinary sort of girl, but occasionally, I see these flashes of spunk and impudence that lead me to believe there is more to her than meets the eye."

His mother smiled at the description. "What does she like to do?"

"I suppose what most young ladies do- shopping, sewing. We have not discussed it much. Oh, but she does enjoy riding, even though she has lacked the means and opportunity to do so."

"She is fortunate, then, that she will soon have the means to make amends for that."

"Yes." Nathaniel remained silent for a few moments, gathering his courage to ask the question that had been plaguing him since he had first written of his impending marriage. "Are you very disappointed in me, Mother?"

She took her time answering him. "Not so much as you have feared, I think. And not so much in the way you think. I am disappointed for your sake, because I had always hoped that you would find love, like your father and I did. I wanted more for you than a marriage of convenience. But convenience can grow into love, with time." She leaned forward to cup his cheek in her hand and gaze lovingly into his eyes. "I look forward to meeting this young woman in the hope that she will be the one to bring you such happiness."

He smiled at his mother's words, feeling a rush of relief. "You shall meet her soon. She is traveling to Town to make some purchases in a few days time. I have arranged to bring her to call on you next Tuesday. I hope that is satisfactory?"

"I should like that very much, Nathaniel."

"I am glad."

He yawned, and his mother smiled. "Go on upstairs to bed. I know it has been a long few days for you. I shall see you in the morning."

He returned her smile and rose to find his valet and his bed.

*****

Kitty's first full day in town had been a marathon of shopping. Her mother never seemed to tire of the warehouses and shops. She was relentless in her pursuit of the best deal and dragged Kitty all over Town. They had returned to the Gardiners late in the evening for a dinner party they were hosting.

Kitty was rather looking forward to the evening, despite her exhaustion after a full day about the Town. Elizabeth and Mr. Darcy were expected to be among the guests, along with Mr. and Mrs. Bingley. She was excited to once again be in the company of the sisters who had had such a strong influence on her. Her fiancé was also expected to make an appearance, providing her an opportunity to introduce him to the most beloved members her family.

She fidgeted in her chair as her aunt's maid tried to coax her curls into subjection.

"Hold still, Miss!"

She stilled obediently and waited patiently for the young woman to finish her work. She barely glanced at the results before slipping into her gown. The dress had been a gift from Elizabeth a few months before, when she had been visiting Pemberley. It was by far the nicest gown she had ever owned, with the exception of a lovely ball gown from Jane that she had yet to have an occasion to wear.

It was bottle-green, to match her eyes and liven her complexion. The neckline was scooped and trimmed with scalloped lace. She ran her fingers lightly over the fine fabric and twirled in front of the mirror to admire the lines and cut of the material. Even knowing that she would pale in comparison to Jane, she still felt more beautiful and fashionable in that dress than she had since the day Lydia had emerged into society and upstaged her.

It was a very cheerful and confident young lady that descended the stairs that evening to greet her sisters.

"Kitty!" Jane exclaimed upon greeting her. "You look radiant! That gown becomes you so! And your hair! You are positively enchanting!"

Kitty giggled and embraced her sister, commenting slyly, "You are glowing yourself. But I do not suppose it is your gown to thank for that."

Jane blushed at the insinuation, but did not deny it. She and Elizabeth were both in the early stages of increasing and had only recently confirmed the additions to their family.

Elizabeth joined them, saying, "Kitty, I do not believe I have ever seen you looking so lovely and grown up."

Kitty blushed at the compliment. The sisters quickly made up for lost time, catching each other up on all the latest news, except for one very important announcement that Kitty conveniently left out.

It was quite a shock then, when the last guest of the evening arrived and was announced. A hush fell over the room and the newcomers to the house turned to stare as Lord Rockingham stepped into the room.

"Whatever is he doing here?" Elizabeth whispered to her sister.

Kitty swallowed hard but managed to respond quite calmly, "He is my fiancé."

Both of her sisters turned to stare at her in surprise, speechless. While they gawked, Mr. Bingley and Mr. Darcy recollected their manners and approached Nathaniel, involving him in conversation.

Recovering from their astonishment, Jane and Elizabeth took Kitty by the elbow and pulled her into an unoccupied corner.

"Whatever do you mean, he is your fiancé!" Lizzy hissed.

"Just that. We are engaged to be married. How is it you do not know? I thought Mamma would have told you the news at once. She certainly broadcasted the fact all through Meryton."

"I cannot fathom how she managed to refrain, but she certainly did not inform me of the fact!" Lizzy said.

"She did not tell me, either," Jane commented. "How did this happen?"

Kitty told the tale reluctantly, fully expecting her sisters to be judgmental. To her surprise, they were not.

"It is just like that ridiculous man," Lizzy complained. "He has always been able to ignore the facts and allow his imagination to take flight, even when the reality is right in front of his face!"

"Poor Kitty," Jane commiserated, "To have to make such a choice! Lord Rockingham seems like an amiable man though. Mayhap you will be very happy together."

Lizzy laughed. "Yes, and Lydia will be quite jealous, for not only have you surpassed her in wealth, but you have gained a title as well! Only watch out that she does not drain you of pin money, as she is sure to apply to you for some aid or another. They never can live within their means."

Kitty took this advice to heart, remembering how often she had loaned Lydia some of her pin money for ribbon or lace with the promise of repayment, only to never see the money again.

"Well, we had best meet this affianced of yours," Lizzy suggested mischievously. "He is very handsome and rich, just as a young man ought to be, but let us see if he is worthy of your hand."

"Much good it will do me," Kitty muttered. "The marriage contract has already been signed." But she allowed her sisters to drag her forward to join the men.

Nathaniel was stunned by the change in his fiancé as she approached. Her eyes were alight with laughter and her cheeks flushed with joy. Her gown fit her perfectly, highlighting her slender figure. She was radiant, confident, all the things he had assumed she was not. What had brought about this transformation?

So consumed was he by these thoughts, he neglected to notice her two companions, whom Darcy sought to introduce to him. The other man had to state his name twice before he finally managed to snatch his attention from his bride-to-be.

"Lord Rockingham, I would like to introduce my wife, Mrs. Darcy, and her sister, Mrs. Bingley."

Elizabeth extended her hand with a smile. "It is a pleasure to meet you, my Lord, and a pleasure to be able to call you Brother. I am sure my husband is greatly relieved to know there will be another voice of reason in the family."

The stoic Darcy actually cracked a smile at this statement, further astounding Nathaniel. This was to be an evening of unexpected occurrences it seemed!

"It is a pleasure to meet you both as well," Nathaniel demurred. "I had not expected to have the honor of making your acquaintance quite so soon upon our arrival in Town. It is quite some time since I have had the privilege of coming upon Mr. Darcy at a social event."

Lizzy laughed. "I can well imagine. Darcy is not one to be at ease in society, but we are practicing this Season for Georgiana's come-out next year. *That* is sure to be a trying exercise."

This was acknowledged to be so by all.

"I do not believe, my Lord, that I am aware of where you call home. Do you reside here in Town?" Jane asked.

Nathaniel could sense her sisterly concern over the well-being of her younger sister in the question. "I do have a townhouse here in Town, but my main residence is my estate, Cheventhorpe, near Rotherham, Yorkshire. I expect that is where Miss Bennet and I shall spend most of our time after our marriage. I, like Darcy, do not much care for the pleasures of Town."

Kitty's ears perked up at this, as it was more information about her future than she had managed to discover on her own.

She asked, "Does Cheventhorpe have a large park?"

Nathaniel was surprised at her interest. "It does. The estate encompasses around ninety thousand acres, but the park itself is one hundred and fifty acres. There are some beautiful woodlands and open fields that make for a pleasant ride."

"It sounds wonderful."

He smiled at her enthusiasm, feeling some warmth toward her at the compliment to his home. "I think it is. I hope you shall feel at home there."

She blushed at his gaze and dropped her eyes.

Bingley cleared his throat at the awkward silence that threatened to stretch between them. "I hope we shall have the pleasure of your company at Chetborn sometime after the wedding. It is quite a distance from Yorkshire, I am aware, but it is within thirty miles of Pemberley, and I am sure we should all make a delightful family party."

Nathaniel was awed by their easy acceptance of him into the family. Lacking any siblings of his own, he had suddenly gained what he had never known he had missed. They all agreed that it sounded like a wonderful plan, and even though no date was decided upon, Nathaniel found himself quite looking forward to the time. Kitty supported the idea as well, being understandably afraid of becoming isolated from her sisters.

They were soon called into dinner, and here the company was much the same. Kitty found herself seated beside Nathaniel. The conversation over the table was pleasant and witty, full of laughter and lively chatter. Nathaniel had found himself at many a dinner party over the years, but never had he attended one so delightfully laid back. The company, while all that was proper, were notably fond of each other and there was a great deal of teasing on everyone's part.

He found himself, being less-acquainted with most of the guests, observing the general cheer about him rather than partaking in it. His attention was especially caught by Kitty, whose vibrancy among the current company lit her features. He had never seen a woman so beautiful as she was here. He could not imagine how he had ever thought her ordinary. Even Jane's celebrated beauty paled in comparison.

She seemed to have forgotten him entirely as her sisters encouraged her and praised her accomplishments. He could scarcely believe that the woman before him was the same who had shared a table with him at Rosings and again at Longbourn. It was a testament to the difference love, acceptance, and attention could make in a person.

The separation of the sexes after dinner was mercifully brief, for many of the men in attendance had no desire to prolong their division from their wives. The rest of the evening passed very agreeably, with lively conversation and pleasant music.

It was with genuine regret that Nathaniel departed, but not before expressing his hope of taking Miss Bennet to call upon his mother the following Tuesday. She became more withdrawn at the suggestion, a flicker of fear appearing in her eyes, but agreed to the excursion.

The agreed upon day arrived, and Kitty found herself pacing the downstairs parlor and obsessively checking her appearance in the mirror every few minutes as she waited. The dress she wore was one of her Sunday best and the lavender color contrasted nicely with her green eyes. Although it had been made over to reflect the latest fashions in Hertfordshire, there was no hiding that it was several years old.

Her bonnet, however, was a recent purchase, and was the one piece in her everyday wardrobe in which she had no shame. She could appear in it without compunction to meet her future mother-in-law. She, in fact, felt quite fetching in it, and had decided to wear it today as a much-needed confidence boost.

Nathaniel, upon arriving, agreed with her assessment of the bonnet. It framed her delicate features nicely, the purple ribbon further bringing out her eyes. His only regret was the necessity of the bonnet at all, for he would have preferred to see her as he first had, hair cascading down her back, throwing propriety to the wind.

The likelihood of that occurring anytime soon, he admitted to himself, was not high.

"You look especially lovely today, Miss Bennet," he complimented her.

She glanced at him in surprise at the compliment and then grinned widely. "Thank you, my Lord."

He was pleased to have garnished such a reaction with just a few simple words. He handed her into the carriage and climbed in afterwards. She stroked the superior fabric of the carriage seat beneath her and cast her eye around the fine interior. She was almost afraid to touch anything; it was so unnerving to be surrounded by such finery.

One would think she would be used to the finer things, having spent so much time with her elder sisters in Derbyshire. But the experiences of her youth had taught her that people did not take kindly to any damage done to their possessions, especially if they were of quality. And as one of five sisters, she had never truly owned anything of value herself to feel comfortable with the idea.

Nathaniel sensed her discomfort in the elegant confines, and sought to distract her thoughts.

"Have you been shopping any more Miss Bennet? Your mother declared her intention to do so upon our last meeting."

"A little," she responded. "My sisters, Jane and Lizzy, have agreed to take me around to some of their favorite shops tomorrow. My mother is to spend the day at home with my Aunt Gardiner in order to rest from her exertions. She has very fragile nerves, you know."

She did not explain that the real reason for this was to give Kitty a break from her mother's incessant meddling, rather than a real need on her mother's part for rest. Her mother's tastes in material and clothing were very similar to Lydia's, gaudy and vulgar. Under her sisters' tutelage, Kitty's tastes had become more refined and elegant, but she had come under increasing pressure from her mother on this trip to conform to her choices. Jane and Lizzy had stepped in to ensure that Kitty got the articles she needed, and wanted, to begin her married life properly.

She was grateful for their intercession, for she was not sure how much longer she would have been able to hold out under her mother's constant comparisons to Lydia and ridicule of her choices.

Nathaniel's voice drew her wavering attention. "I am sure your sisters will be able to help you make suitable choices."

She smiled at his tactful words, sensing that he had understood what she had left unsaid. "I am sure they will. Our tastes are very similar. And as two recently married ladies themselves, they have many practical suggestions."

"You are fortunate then, to have someone to guide you. I have found myself often wishing in the past weeks for someone to advise me in the proper decorum for our situation."

She laughed lightly. "I do not think there are rules to govern our circumstances. We shall just have to make them up as we go along."

He smiled at her statement, glad for the lighthearted moment between them. He leaned forward to take her hands between his. She jerked in surprise at his touch, but did not pull away.

"Miss Bennet," he began earnestly, "I know our situation is not optimal. I am sure that like I, you had always hoped to marry for love. But now that we find ourselves in this situation, let us make the best of it. I hope we may become friends, if nothing else."

Kitty smiled at the unexpected words. This was a side of her future husband that she not seen before and she found it surprisingly touching. He had offered her a glimmer of hope for the future, and it sparked a small flame of warmth in her toward him. "I should like that very much, my Lord."

He leaned back, releasing her hands with an answering smile. "Then, as your friend, I must insist that you call me Nathaniel when we are alone. This "My Lord" business is ridiculous. None of my closest associates have ever referred to me as such, and I shall not allow my wife do so."

"I shall do my best to remember that."

"Are you not going to allow me the same liberties?" he asked with mock hurt.

"I do not know," she responded with a teasing glint in her eye. "I have never been a Marchioness before. Perhaps I shall enjoy the use of my titles."

He laughed and she relented. "My given name is Catherine, but my family has always called me Kitty. You may refer to me however you like."

He studied her with sudden seriousness. "Catherine is too staid a name for someone with such joie de vivre, and yet Kitty is too juvenile." His eyes lit up. "I think I have the perfect compromise, if you are willing to allow it."

She raised an eyebrow at this supposition, but withheld judgment. She rather liked his description of her. Mayhap he did not view her as so ordinary after all.

"How do you feel about the name Kate?" Nathaniel asked, a little hesitantly. She mulled the name over in her head before giving him her approval. She had been called many worse things in her life. Who was she to deny him the pleasure of calling her what he chose? Besides, it really did seem to fit her. She felt more like a lady just thinking of herself as Kate rather than Kitty.

The carriage pulled up in front of Nathaniel's townhouse, and they exited with a new resolve and an ease between them that had not existed before.

Still, Kitty felt a jolt of discomfort as Nathaniel handed her out of the carriage and she looked up at the grand home before her. She took a deep breath to calm herself. The Darcy's townhouse was every bit as grand and elegant as this. It was no different. But it was still such a foreign world to her. She had never truly belonged among such opulence. She had always been a guest, a visitor, with the knowledge that she would return to her humble origins when the duration of her stay had run its course.

Within those walls was her future mother-in-law, a woman who by all accounts was as grand and elegant as her surroundings. The butterflies in Kitty's stomach took a nosedive.

Nathaniel smiled kindly at her, and tucked her hand in his arm. The trembling of her fingers belied her nerves as they took the stairs. The servants' faces were a blur as they passed, although she was aware of the whispers that followed them. What they must think of her, a mere country gentleman's daughter, here among the peerage!

Before she knew it, they were standing in front of the parlor doors, ready to be admitted. When the doors swung open, she entered on shaky legs, observing a beautiful older woman rise to meet them.

She came forward with a gentle smile to greet her son.

"Hello, Mother. I would like to introduce my betrothed, Miss Catherine Bennet of Longbourn. Kate, this is my mother, the Marchioness of Rockingham."

Kate curtsied deeply. "It is a pleasure to meet you, Lady Rockingham."

"Soon to be the Dowager Lady Rockingham," she said with a smile, taking Kitty's hands in her own. "But there is no need to stand on ceremony among family. Please, call me Cecelia, Miss Bennet. I am very glad to meet you."

She gestured for them to all take a seat. "I have been very anxious to learn more about my new daughter. Nathaniel has told me very little about you."

Kitty blushed. "I am afraid we have had very little opportunity to get to know one another."

"Hmmm…" Cecelia murmured. "I believe my son has neglected his duty to court you. Tell me, how many times has he called on you since you have arrived in Town?"

The tips of Nathaniel's ears turned red in embarrassment and he began, "Now, Mother, I have been very…"

She cut him off with a wave of her hand. "Excuses, Nathaniel. How many times, Miss Bennet?"

Kate grinned at the sudden reversal of their roles. "Just the once."

Cecelia tsked. "Nathaniel, must I remind you of your duties as a gentleman? You must never neglect your lady. A happy wife is a happy life, as I often told your father."

Nathaniel grumbled under his breath at being reduced to a petulant school boy by his mother, instead of as the capable man he was, but did not dare to correct her. At least Kate seemed to be enjoying the attack on him.

In fact, it was a calculated effort on Cecelia's part to put the young lady at ease, and to remind her son of his own fine upbringing. The young man was far too arrogant sometimes for his own good.

"Now, Miss Bennet, do tell me a little about yourself."

"Please, call me Catherine."

The next half hour passed in pleasant conversation. Cecelia found her companion to be intelligent and witty, and enjoyed their time together immensely. Kitty likewise found herself to be quite comfortable in the Marchioness' company. The older woman was as elegant as the reports had made her out to be, but she was also remarkably down to earth and level-headed. Nathaniel had watched their interaction with contentment, a pleasant fore-gleam of the domestic felicity to come.

He saw his bride back to her aunt's with an invitation to the opera later that night. It was time to take their betrothal public. As much as he loathed exposing her to the prying eyes of the Ton, he needed to admit that he was officially off the Market. It was a way to show Kate his confidence in her as the next Marchioness of Rockingham.

*****

Kitty stepped out of the carriage that night to the twinkling lights and glamour of the opera all around her. The crush of people was both thrilling and frightening. She was excited to be counted among one of those privileged to be there to enjoy the musical experience. Never in her life had she thought to be able to enjoy such splendor.

Her family had never had the means to fund a trip to Town, much less to dress five daughters for the opera, and her father certainly had never had the inclination. He was happy enough at home, among his books and philosophers. It would never have occurred to him that some among his daughters would have relished the opportunity.

Kitty could not help the small smile that spread across her face when she thought of how jealous Lydia would be when she heard. It was perhaps petty of her to so enjoy her sister's loss, but the act was justified by Lydia's many taunts, especially over her trip to Brighton.

Nathaniel noticed the smile but had no time to comment on it, as he was far too busy trying to shove his way through the crowds while maintaining a vigilant eye for pick-pockets. He was relieved to leave the crowds behind them as they arrived at their box. He pulled the heavy velvet curtain closed and went to sit near the front with his mother and Kitty. They were already occupied comparing the many beautiful gowns on display.

"I particularly like that azure satin. The gathering on the bodice is beautiful!" Kitty pointed out to Cecelia.

"Hmmm… Yes," Cecelia agreed. "That color would look wonderful on you. You will have a whole new sphere of choices to choose from once you are married." She glanced at the box across from them. "Oh, my. That is an obscene amount of décolletage on Mrs. Rycroft! Take my advice, Catherine. A true lady never reveals too much skin."

Kitty readily agreed.

"Now there is a gorgeous gown! Do you see, just there?"

Nathaniel leaned back in his seat to just listen contentedly as the two ladies went on. Eventually, the lights dimmed and the performance began. While Kitty found the music enthralling, she enjoyed it more for the experience than for any real interest in the art form. Her knowledge of music was perfunctory at best.

Nathaniel discovered this upon intermission. His shock was short-lived as he recalled a certain conversation with Lady Catherine that should have prepared him for this eventuality. While in his experience every young lady was brought up with a knowledge of opera and music, in her household this had not been the case. His mother did not seem to be concerned with her lack of experience and knowledge, instead claiming that the main reason to attend was to see and be seen anyway.

Intermission also brought guests to the box, as by this time, many had noticed the presence of a certain unknown young lady. Kitty became uncomfortably aware of the pointed stares and whispers, but tried to maintain a cool and collected outward visage as the first visitors gathered their courage enough to stop by their box.

The lady watched her with hungry, bird-like eyes that kept darting between her and Nathaniel, while the older gentleman's gaze raked roguishly over her figure.

Nathaniel greeted them with a calm that Kitty could not understand. "Mr. and Mrs. Dobney, how good of you to stop by. I do not believe you have met my fiancée, Miss Catherine Bennet."

Kate stood for the introductions with as much graciousness and tact as she could muster. "It is a pleasure to make your acquaintance."

Mrs. Dobney sniffed and raised her chin, replying haughtily, "Likewise, I am sure."

The couple moved on quite quickly after that, absconding to a few boxes down to whisper feverishly with its occupants.

Nathaniel chuckled. "Well, that should get the gossips going."

"Your name and family will be known all over Town by morning," Cecelia observed. "Unfortunately, that also means the tale of your, how shall we say it, close encounter, will probably spread as well."

Kitty frowned. "I cannot understand why anyone would concern themselves with me. I am not terribly interesting."

Cecelia replied, "You are to be the next Lady Rockingham, my dear. There are many young women who would have liked that title for themselves. Once you are married, they will not dare to ridicule you, and this shall all blow over. But until then, I would watch your back. The Marriage Mart can be quite the cutthroat place."

Kitty nodded slowly and turned to glance up to where the Dobneys were standing. The evil glares sent her way were enough to convince her of the truth of Lady Rockingham's words.

London, it seemed, was not such a nice place after all.

CHAPTER FIVE

Kitty was glad to leave London behind her. What had begun as a fun and exciting change of pace had degraded into a tense and taxing ordeal. She could not regret the opportunities that London had provided her to visit with her sisters and meet Lady Rockingham, but it was not the town she had thought it to be. Everywhere she went after attending the opera, people would recognize her, and the whispers and giggles would start. No one had been so overt as to say anything to her face, but she knew what was being said about her behind her back.

The rumors circulating mostly held that she had seduced Lord Rockingham like some common harlot, and now she was "increasing" and he was being forced to marry her.

Kitty found the rumors to be hurtful. Her reputation was in shatters, but her marriage to Nathaniel would quiet the gossip, especially once enough time had passed to rule out a pregnancy on her part. No, it was the belief that she would actually do such a thing that hurt her more than anything. True, these people had no foreknowledge of her and her personality, but surely what was being said in Town were only echoes of what was being said about her in Hertfordshire.

It was just too unbelievable that she, *Kitty Bennet*, would catch a Marquess on her own merits. And the sad fact of the matter, she had to admit to herself, was that it was true! The only reason Nathaniel had offered for her was because he had compromised her. He would not have been interested in her as a marriage partner any other way.

She breathed a sigh of relief as London faded in the distance and the countryside appeared around them. The rumors might follow her to Hertfordshire, but the wedding was to take place in two weeks time. She would not have long to face their condemnation. And by marrying by special license, only those who truly knew her character would be in attendance. There would not be anyone that would judge her.

Within the day, she was once again safely ensconced within the four walls of her own room in Longbourn. She did not have long to occupy it as a single woman, and she found herself oddly nostalgic upon her return. She had never thought to feel such fondness for a home she had never truly felt she had belonged in. But now that she was faced with leaving it behind her for the unknown, the familiar house held appeal.

Nathaniel and Cecelia arrived in Hertfordshire the Thursday before the wedding was to take place and the Darcys and the Bingleys arrived soon thereafter. That same day, an unexpected missive arrived from Mrs. Wickham. Kitty read it tentatively, a sense of dread overcoming her.

'My Dear Kitty,

I could scarce contain my laughter upon receiving your last letter. What a lark! To jest about marrying a Marquess! The very thought of such an event even now sends me into peals! At first, I was unconvinced of your impending nuptials at all, thinking you to be only teasing me, but Mamma has assured me that you are, in fact, to be married. I admit I am more than a little curious about my future brother, and so I have decided to surprise you! My dear Wickham is unable to accompany me, but I shall be arriving on Tuesday for your wedding! I know you shall be ecstatic to see me, as it has been ages since we were last together! Dreadful Pappa never would allow you to visit me, even though I should have found you a husband twice as handsome I am sure. But we shall meet again on Tuesday! Your affectionate sister,

Mrs. Lydia Wickham"

Kitty noted ironically the delight her sister took in signing her name "Mrs. Lydia Wickham," by the number of swirls and flourishes she used. Lydia may not have wanted to believe her sister was truly marrying a Marquess, but she had been startled enough to make the trip to find out the truth.

Kitty was not looking forward to her presence.

*****

They were quite a large party that gathered in the parlor to await Lydia's arrival. Mrs. Bennet had seated herself in such a way as to have a clear view out the window in anticipation of her youngest daughter's coming. Mr. Bennet was quite happily involved in a lively discussion with his favorite daughter and her husband in one corner, while Mary and Georgiana did their best to entertain them all with some light tunes on the pianoforte in the other.

Jane and Bingley were settled on the settee, with Kitty, Nathaniel, and Cecelia seated around them. Their discussion was light and pleasant, as any conversation involving the Bingleys is bound to be, but Kitty was wound tight with nervous anxiety.

Nathaniel noticed her fidgeting in her seat and the constant straying of her gaze to the window and the drive beyond. At first, he had assumed that her inattention was the result of sisterly affection and a longing to be within Lydia's company, but her cool demeanor and agitated motions had soon convinced him of the contrary. Still, he could not understand why the appearance of a sister should be the cause of such apprehension. He had not long to wait to find out.

The crunch of gravel on the drive heralded her, and Mrs. Bennet jumped up, crying, "She is come- my dear Lydia is come!"

Lydia's voice was soon heard in the vestibule; the door was thrown open, and she ran into the room. Her mother stepped forward, embraced her, and welcomed her with rapture. Her reception from Mr. Bennet, while cordial, was not so warm. Lydia then turned to her sisters, unabashed in her effusions, despite the presence of company. She was introduced to Georgiana, and exclaimed over the young lady's gown to such a degree as to bring a blush to that shy lady's cheeks.

At length, she deigned to notice the presence of her sister's beau and his mother.

"Oh! La! Kitty! You have forgotten to introduce me!" she cried with a giggle, and put out her hand to Nathaniel. He took the proffered member with some displeasure at her manners and bowed over it as Kitty performed the introductions.

"Lord Rockingham, Lady Rockingham, this is my youngest sister, Mrs. Lydia Wickham. Lydia, this is my betrothed, Lord Rockingham, and his mother, Lady Rockingham, of Cheventhorpe."

Lydia started at this proclamation. "So it is true then. You really are marrying a Marquess!"

Kitty flushed at the outburst and glanced at Nathaniel, an apology in her eyes. He was stunned by Lydia's unseemly display, but tried to hide it as he could tell Kate was already distressed by her sister's actions.

"Yes, I assure you it is true, Mrs. Wickham," he said slowly.

She seemed to flounder for a moment before breaking out in a bright smile. "La! How silly of me! I should have known Kitty would not jest about who her husband is. She never has known how to have fun! *I* was always the one everyone wanted around."

Nathaniel would not have been surprised if the jab had been followed by a stuck-out tongue, it was so juvenile.

"I am not surprised that those among *your* circles find you amusing, Mrs. Wickham," Lady Rockingham said coolly.

Lydia ignored the reprimand in her voice and the implied slight. Lydia was Lydia still- untamed, unabashed, wild, noisy, and fearless. She, who never heard nor saw anything of which she chose to be insensible, gaily continued, joining their small group, much to the consternation of all concerned.

"Why, even Mrs. Forster asked me to come to Brighton as her most particular friend. And what a lark that was!"

Lydia continued on in like vein, and once Mrs. Bennet joined them, there could be no lack of discourse. Mother and daughter could neither of them talk fast enough.

At length, a walk about the garden was suggested and eagerly took up by most of the party. Here at least there was some relief, as Mrs. Bennet required her favorite daughter to attend her in the parlor. Mr. Bennet escaped to his study with some hurried excuse, and the rest departed for the outdoors.

The walk was wide enough for two or three abreast, and the party quickly broke down into smaller groups. Lady Rockingham found herself soon at the head of the party with Georgiana Darcy on one side and Mary Bennet on the other. The two young ladies, she found, shared a love of music; and despite a propensity on both their sides to be withdrawn, she was soon able to draw them out on the subject.

Mr. and Mrs. Bingley and Mr. and Mrs. Darcy paired off as quickly as possible, leaving Kitty and Nathaniel to follow behind. Kitty was not so great a walker as her sisters, and they were very shortly outpaced.

Nathaniel could not complain. Since Kitty had departed London, the demands on both of their time had increased exponentially as the wedding date approached. His own wedding preparations and then the arrival of her family at Longbourn had prevented him from spending any time alone in her company. They had not had the opportunity for private conversation in weeks. He was surprised to find that he missed the time they spent in each other's company.

He opened the discussion eagerly. "Tell me, Kate, have you been as overwhelmed with wedding preparations as I have been? I never knew there was so much involved in preparing to enter the matrimonial state!"

She laughed lightly at his statement. "Yes, it is quite taxing, is it not? I am quite grateful for the arrival of Jane and Lizzy. They have been very helpful in distracting my mother from her constant anxiety over the wedding. Now that Lydia has arrived I shall not be bothered by her for an opinion over three or four times per day, I should think." She tilted her head to peer up at him. "I do not understand why she bothers to ask my opinion anyway, for she very rarely takes it into account when she makes a decision. I would much rather be spared her attention."

He covered her hand on his arm with his own and smiled down at her. "It is good, then, that you do not have much longer to worry about that."

She was discomfited by his warm smile and soft touch and broke his gaze, dropping her head to watch where they were walking. Nathaniel noticed her withdrawal and reluctantly removed his hand from hers, an unexpected twinge of disappointment coursing through him at her reaction.

"Yes, only a few more days and then I shall be free from my mother's attentions; although she has assured me repeatedly she shall write and guide me in my duties as a wife. So perhaps I shall not be entirely free after all," she noted with a stiff smile.

Nathaniel sighed to himself. It was difficult to acknowledge the wall that still stood between them. One moment they could be conversing as easy-going acquaintances, the next they were back to being as stiff and formal as at their first association. Would things never change?

"It is difficult for any parent to acknowledge their child has grown up and no longer needs their protection and guidance. I thought my father would never allow me to be my own man, but then when he passed away, I found I missed his interfering ways. In his own way, he was trying to show he cared for me, I think. It is funny how we fail to appreciate those things until it is too late."

Nathaniel's heartfelt words brought her gaze back to his face. She squeezed his arm sympathetically. "I am sorry for your loss, Nathaniel. I apologize if my words seemed cavalier. I am fortunate, indeed, that I still have both of my parents around to complain about."

He accepted her words with a nod, resisting the urge to cover her hand with his own again. In revealing a little of himself to her, he hoped to draw her out in turn. They could not remain acquaintances forever. Although they had vowed to be friends, they had yet to attain to that depth of a relationship. There was too much unsaid between them yet. If they ever were to have the friendly relationship he hoped for, they would need to open themselves up and trust each other. They still had a long way to go.

"Let us speak of happier topics," he suggested. "Tell me about yourself as a little girl. There must have been many adventures, growing up in a household with five daughters."

Kate laughed and began to tell him some silly tale about a mishap with the family cat. She was an accomplished story-teller, he found to his surprise, and he could hear the genuine love and warmth in her voice that she held for her family, despite their many shortcomings.

Her upbringing may not have been what was traditional, but he could not find fault with it when it had produced the woman standing before him now.

Nathaniel could not help but reflect that her story-telling would be much in demand when their children came along. He could picture them, a motley mix of young boys and girls, gathered around her skirts to listen as she wove them some dramatic tale.

The mental image was a compelling one, and he had to swallow passed a lump in his throat to comment on her anecdote. He had, up until this point, never dwelled on the possibility of children between them. It seemed too far-fetched a reality when they were barely able to carry on a conversation. Even though children were still far in the future, he found he liked the idea of having them with Kate.

"It sounds like you had a delightful childhood," he acknowledged with a grin.

"I think so," she said with a laugh.

"I look forward to many more of your stories in the years to come."

"There are certainly plenty to share." Her eyes twinkled merrily at the thought and he could not help but reflect on the very great pleasure which a pair of fine eyes in the face of a pretty woman can bestow.

He made a mental note to have a portrait commissioned once they were married that would do justice to those beautiful eyes. It would not be easy to catch their expression, but their color and shape, and the eyelashes, so remarkably fine, might be copied.

"Surely you must have some amusing anecdotes from your own childhood to share," she teased, drawing his attention back from his wandering thoughts.

"Very few, I am afraid," he admitted, a little embarrassed. "I was much of a loner as a child. I had no other siblings to goad me on, and my father insisted I not mingle with any of the tenants' children. It was not until I went away to school that I learned the joy of a well-played prank."

"Well then, you must tell me what it was like at school."

He did so gladly, happy to amuse her at his own expense. It was pure joy to see her smile, her eyes lit with laughter. So passed the remainder of the time until dinner, when they were obliged to return to the house.

There were only a few days now until the wedding was to take place, and they were unremarkable in their passing. Much had to be accomplished before the blessed event could take place, but with the addition of Lizzy and Jane, the load was made lighter, and the days passed quickly.

*****

The morning of her wedding dawned bright, giving Kitty a reason to rejoice. A gray, dreary day would have been a poor send off for a bride indeed.

She was up early to oversee the packing of the last of her things. Unfortunately, Lydia was up uncharacteristically early as well. She let herself into Kitty's room and threw herself across the bed on her stomach.

"You are up early this morning, Lydia," Kitty commented, wondering what her sister was up to.

"Mamma was bustling about already and I found it quite a trial to sleep with such noise! Besides, I wanted to see all your pretty new things before they were all packed away."

She got to her feet and started pawing through one of the trunks, disrupting the tidy packing. She pulled out some ribbons and held them up to admire them.

"Oh! These are lovely! Do say I can have them Kitty! You will have lots of nice things once you are married and Wickham and I can never afford such fine things. Think of the pin money you shall have! You will not even miss these!"

Kitty sighed. It was not worth the hassle for a few ribbons. "Go ahead, take them."

Lydia giggled and twirled around with the ribbons before retiring to the bed to admire her booty.

The time flew by quickly, and before she knew it, it was time to start getting dressed. The entire household was up by this time and bustling, everyone flitting from one room to the next and from one task to another. Hill was helping her into her stays when Lydia stumbled upon another item she desired.

"Oh! Those slippers are divine, Kitty!" Lydia picked up the slippers to look at them more closely. The bottle-green slippers had been specially ordered to match Kitty's wedding dress. While the dress would most likely be worn until it fell to pieces, she meant to save the slippers as a memento of the day. It was not everyday a girl got married, after all.

Lydia looked up with bright eyes, and Kitty could tell where this was headed.

"No! Lydia! No, you cannot have those!" Kitty cried as Lydia backed toward the door, trying unsuccessfully to snatch the slippers out of her sister's grasp. Her heart lurched at the sight of the slippers, dangling from Lydia's fingers tauntingly.

Their mother appeared in the doorway at the bustle.

"What is going on in here?!" Mrs. Bennet asked. "Your father is not to be disturbed this morning!"

Lydia immediately turned to her mother, recognizing an old ally, and pleaded, "Mamma, tell Kitty to let me have these slippers. They are so beautiful, and she will have so many fine things, while I have none. Please, Mamma!"

Mrs. Bennet wavered, sending Kitty an apologetic glance, before giving in to her favorite's request. "Perhaps just this once. Surely you would not mind, Kitty. You will have many pairs of slippers once you are married."

Kitty's mouth hung open, aghast. "But, Mamma! Those are mine!"

Lydia had already started edging past Mrs. Bennet, her face triumphant, when suddenly Lizzy appeared in the doorway and snatched the slippers from her grasp.

"Mamma! It is Kitty's wedding day! You cannot mean—but you do! For shame! This is ridiculous!" Lizzy scolded them, shooing them out of the room. "Leave Kitty in peace!"

She closed the door on the madness and smiled gently at her younger sister in the mirror. She handed over the slippers. "I would keep a close eye on these if I were you."

Kitty laughed shakily and took them gratefully, holding them close against her chest. Hill finished tying her stays and excused herself.

"These slippers are the one thing I have to cherish of today," she explained. "Pappa told me he had them dyed especially to match my dress and my eyes. I could not bear to see Lydia have them. They would be soiled within the week."

"I know," Lizzy murmured. "Lydia never took care of her things. And a woman's wedding day is something to be cherished. Today is your day. Do not let Lydia ruin it for you."

She stepped forward to hug Kitty before smiling widely. "Now, there is still much to be done. Let me help you into your gown."

The two sisters spent the next few hours in pleasant companionship as they finished readying for the wedding. Lizzy was always a lively companion, and Kitty enjoyed their time together immensely, as she knew she was unlikely to see her sister again for some time. Lizzy would be retiring to Pemberley for her confinement soon, and Jane would likewise be constrained to Chetborn.

She would miss their constant presence in her life and their good advice. She was certainly going to want it as she adjusted to her new role.

At precisely eleven o'clock, she descended the stairs to meet her groom, with her sisters to attend her. They were married with a special license in her childhood home, with only their family and Mr. and Mrs. Fitzwilliam in attendance. She wore bottle-green and he wore a dove gray coat.

Mrs. Bennet could be heard remarking that Catherine looked almost as beautiful as Jane had on her wedding day. She could hardly contain her joy at having a fourth daughter married, and to a Marquess at that! She blubbered through the ceremony, wildly fluttering her handkerchief and crying tears of ecstatic joy. To have a peer of the realm in the family!

After the short ceremony, the family adjourned to the dining room for the wedding breakfast. Mrs. Bennet had gone to great lengths to have Meryton's finest set on her table. She had spent hours haggling with the butcher and baker for the best cuts and had directed the cook minutely in the preparation of the white soup.

She beamed with pleasure upon receiving Lord Rockingham's compliments on the meal and proceeded to give him a long-winded explanation of the various choices she had made.

Kitty, feeling some compassion for her new husband upon observing his bewildered expression, interrupted the monologue with the suggestion that it was time they were away.

Nathaniel, relieved at the interruption, hastily agreed. They were seen off without much fanfare. Many of the guests also had long journeys ahead of them and were eager to be off. Lady Rockingham was to return to Town for a fortnight before joining them at Cheventhorpe. The Bingleys and the Darcys were traveling north to their country estates, not to be removed from them for many months. Lydia was to stay for a fortnight at Longbourn, but then she too would be departing for Newcastle. Only Mary was to remain at home.

The atmosphere in Nathaniel and Kitty's coach quickly went from relieved to awkward as they passed from the view of their families. Neither Lord nor Lady had any idea how to comport themselves with each other now that they were married.

Kitty avoided eye contact by staring out the window under the pretense of watching the countryside go by. The silence stretched between them for some time before Nathaniel tried to bridge it.

He cleared his throat. "The journey to Yorkshire will take a couple days. I have made arrangements for us to stay at a very pleasant coaching inn along the way."

Kitty reluctantly made eye contact. "I am sure whatever accommodations you have made will suffice."

"We will be stopping in Grantham. They are very well known for their gingerbread there. You must try some tonight during dinner. They also have a not-so-charming little tradition of an annual pig drive right through the centre of town. Thankfully, *that* will not be occurring during our stay."

She wrinkled her nose distastefully. "I should think that would be monstrously unpleasant."

"I imagine so," Nathaniel commented. "As I have always avoided the town at that time of year, I cannot tell you for sure."

She smiled at his statement, and the tension eased slightly between them.

"Do you enjoy gingerbread?" she ventured.

He smiled and replied in the affirmative, sparking a conversation on various preferences that saw them to the outskirts of Grantham.

The inn they finally disembarked at was as charming as Nathaniel had made it out to be. It was clean and well-kept, and the inn-keeper's wife had gone to great pains to make the rustic exterior as appealing as possible. She had large flower pots set on either side of the entrance, and window boxes overflowing with plants hung at all the first floor windows.

The courtyard was bustling with hostlers and grooms leading horses to their stables. The ring of the blacksmith's hammer could be faintly heard over the din of horses whinnying and men calling out to one another. Kitty was much too enthralled with her surroundings to notice the men that stopped to turn and stare in her wake, but Nathaniel was not so absorbed. He scowled and tucked her hand more firmly in his arm as they passed.

She turned to him with a wide smile. "It is just as charming as you made it out to be!"

He managed to smile tightly back at her. "I am glad it pleases you."

He hurried her inside, eager to get her away from all the male attention she was garnishing. Kitty was surprised by his sudden rush, and a little disappointed, as she was always eager to explore new places.

She had not often had the opportunity to travel, and when the chance did arise, she always wanted to make the most of it. She would have gladly gone for a stroll down the main street and looked in the shops, but her husband was busily occupied escorting her to the private parlor that he had reserved for them.

She frowned at him as the innkeeper's wife closed the door behind her, and then turned to stride to the window, her sudden silence expressing her displeasure.

Nathaniel sighed and crossed the room to join her at the window. For a few moments they both contemplated the gardens displayed before them, before Nathaniel broke the silence.

"It is a pretty country, is it not?"

Kitty frowned and snapped petulantly, "I would not know, since I am apparently not to see it personally."

She turned away from him and flounced to a nearby settee. He followed her across the room and took the seat beside her, even as she ignored him studiously.

He resigned himself to the fact that he was going to have to let her see the town, regardless of the stares she garnered. It was his fault he had chosen such a lively bride. Why could he not have ruined some shy, retiring miss that would prefer to be holed away inside?

"If you would like, we could take a stroll before supper," he offered reluctantly.

He was rewarded with a wide smile and they immediately set off. She took his arm as they walked, humming a little to herself under her breath and occasionally breaking out with a skip. Her enthusiasm was tangible and contagious. Nathaniel felt his own spirits lift as they neared the row of shops that lined the main street of Grantham.

She eagerly stopped to peer in the windows of the first shop they came to. It was a small bookshop, and apparently something inside caught her attention, as she pulled him inside to explore further. Nathaniel was unimpressed with the selection, but waited patiently as his new bride perused the bookshelves.

He was surprised when she plucked a tome from the shelves. He peered over her shoulder to make out the title.

"Mansfield Park?" he asked incredulously. "Her last book was well received, but this one has not garnered any attention from the critics. Why would you want that one?"

She scowled at his comments, but did not put the book back. "Elizabeth recommended it." She held the book a little tighter and lifted her chin defiantly, looking him in the eyes. "Besides, I thought it might be nice to have as a token from our wedding day. It can go in the library as a keepsake for future generations."

He had not expected the emotional attachment she had made to such an insignificant item. Her words silenced his objections immediately. It *would* be a nice gesture to have a small memento of the day.

He took the tome from her hand with a sigh and admitted begrudgingly, "You are right, of course. Is there anything else that you would like?"

She shook her head, a small smile stealing across her face and followed him to the counter as he made the purchase. He had the small package sent back to the inn and they continued down the street, peering in the shop windows. Nothing else particularly caught their eye until they passed a milliner's shop almost at the end of the lane. There was a jaunty little straw bonnet, trimmed in a lovely green that Nathaniel could tell had caught his wife's eye, even if she had yet to admit it.

"Are you going to go inside for a closer look?" he asked curiously.

"No. I have just had a new bonnet while in London." She sighed wistfully over the accessory and made to continue down the street. But Nathaniel stopped her with a hand on her arm.

"But I thought you liked it?" he asked, confused by her actions. In his experience, no woman ever turned down the opportunity to purchase more clothing or headgear.

She turned to him with something akin to bafflement. "I do. But I do not need it."

He felt the idiot as the light suddenly dawned on her actions. Of course as one of five daughters she had felt the strain of the family finances. If the amount her father had settled upon her in the marriage settlements was any indication, her pin money in a year had probably been less than he would spend on a new pair of coach horses without a second thought.

The amount Nathaniel had agreed to settle upon her himself was sizable, but he had the sudden epiphany that while her father had been privy to those documents, Kate herself had never seen them. She had no way of knowing that the funds available to her were vastly larger.

He was ashamed of himself for not noticing the oversight sooner. Once they were settled at Cheventhorpe he was going to have an honest discussion with her about their finances. Until then, far be it from him to deny his wife the simple luxury of a bonnet she did not need.

Wife. It was strange how the simple word changed so much. She was under his protection now. It was his responsibility to make sure she was cared for properly and felt no want. And he was going to make sure she was cared for in a way he doubted anyone had ever done for her before.

He opened the door to the shop and pulled her in after him.

"What are you doing?!" she hissed under her breath at him as he stopped beside the bonnet display. Nathaniel eyed the curious shopkeeper behind the counter angrily, and the woman quickly found something to occupy herself with in the back room.

"My finances are not so straitened that I cannot afford to buy my wife a bonnet," he whispered back, a trace of anger at himself resonating in his voice.

"But I told you, I do not need it," she said in confusion. "My other bonnet is perfectly serviceable, and you told me once that it was very flattering."

"I did, and I still think it is," Nathaniel responded. "But I want you to enjoy nice things. We are perfectly able to afford them, and I would see you happy."

She was touched by his words and smiled up at him, squeezing his arm gently before she let go to examine the bonnet closer. She peered at the stitching and lining closely before trying the item on and turning to ask him flirtatiously, "Well, my Lord, what do you think? Does it suit me?"

He laughed and stepped closer to still the loose ribbons that dangled beneath her chin. "Yes, my Lady, it is very fetching on you."

Their eyes caught and held for a breathless moment, the attraction between them palpable, before they both turned away awkwardly.

Nathaniel stepped back and cleared his throat, withdrawing to examine a selection of goods by the counter. Kitty fiddled with the bonnet ribbons for a few moments more, ostensibly admiring her reflection in the window before she removed the item and joined Nathaniel at the counter, bonnet in hand.

"Have you decided then?" he asked his wife, avoiding her eyes.

"Yes. I should like it very much."

The shopkeeper reappeared magically at her words, leaving Nathaniel with the strong suspicion she had been listening at the door. He paid for his wife's selection and arranged for its delivery before they set off to finish their stroll.

CHAPTER SIX

Upon their return to the inn, they both retired to their rooms to refresh themselves before descending to the private dining room Nathaniel had reserved for their use. They were silent as they waited for the staff to lay out the meal and exit the room.

It was obvious to Kitty from the selection laid upon the table that Nathaniel was used to dining in style. There were many dishes that she had only rarely seen upon the Bennet table, due to their expense. And the sheer number and variety of dishes before them was staggering. There must have been ten separate serving platters expertly arranged before them.

She served herself from the dishes nearest to her and fell to eating, suddenly ravenous. The long journey and the emotional rollercoaster she had been on that day fueled her appetite. Nathaniel watched her with some amusement before turning to his own plate.

He asked, tongue-in-cheek, "Is the mutton to your satisfaction?"

She looked up at him from over her plate and flashed him a smile. "Perfectly so."

He let her continue her meal in peace for some time, as it was evident she had far more interest in her plate at the moment than she did in him. When the platters before them were exhausted and their plates clean, they removed to the parlor with their coffee.

The conversation was light and superfluous. Neither had a desire to mar the harmony that had sprung up between them with any controversial topics. At length, when Nathaniel noticed several suppressed yawns on Kitty's part, he suggested they retire for the night, which Kitty readily agreed to.

He escorted her to her door and saw her secured behind it before entering his own connecting chamber. He sank into a chair near the fireplace and loosened his cravat with one hand, his gaze on the door that stood between him and his wife.

He admitted to himself the appeal his young bride held. She was lively and full of laughter, and almost since the very first time he had met her, he had considered her as one of the handsomest women of his acquaintance.

He was wise enough to know that right now that door was not open to him. It would most likely be quite some time before it represented an invitation instead of a barrier.

Finally, he admitted that his empty bed held no attraction for him that night, so he rose and poured himself a glass of brandy from the sideboard. It was going to be a long night.

*****

Kitty, for her part, had her own ruminations to ponder that night. She allowed the maid to help her out of her gown and into her nightdress, before dismissing her in favor of her own company.

She settled herself on the bed and began to coax a brush through her unruly tresses as she allowed her mind to roam. Their intense encounter in the milliner's shop that afternoon had reminded Kitty of a fact she had unsuccessfully tried to repress during her acquaintance with her husband.

She finally allowed herself to admit openly the attraction she felt towards Nathaniel. His insult had caused her to bury those feelings under her expressed contempt and disdain, but now, privy to his kindness and courtesy towards her, those long suppressed feelings were beginning to bubble up towards the surface.

She felt innately the danger of allowing those feelings to show. Their newfound ease with each other could only be threatened by such open manifestations, as was attested to by their encounter in the shop.

The awkwardness that had ensued was palpable and had lasted until well afterwards. No, it was better that Nathaniel was not aware of her attraction if they were to remain friends in this marriage.

With this newfound intention, she put down the brush and quickly plaited her hair into a long braid over her shoulder before blowing out the candles and crawling under the covers.

*****

They both rose early the next morning and broke their fast at the inn before beginning the last leg of the journey. Nathaniel's eagerness to return home was obvious, as was his desire to show it off to his new bride.

As they neared the grounds, he sat up straighter in his seat, peering out the window and relating any places of interest to Kate. His eagerness was matched by her innate curiosity in what was to be her new home. The little he had told her had been insufficient for her active imagination.

He marked the point where his lands began with a comment, but it was still some time before they turned down the lane to the park, as the estate was quite expansive. The carriage slowed as they neared the house itself, and finally stopped as they crested a hill, revealing the manor before them.

Nathaniel handed his wife out of the coach and led her to the spot overlooking her new home so she could survey the property to her heart's content.

She let out a short bark of laughter as the full façade of the house unfolded before her and the panic set in. This was to be her home? Over all this she was to be mistress? If only Lydia could see her now! The very thought was daunting.

The great house laid before her must have been three times the size of Pemberley. The exterior was clothed in the Baroque style, with wings extending evenly from either side of the original manor in the Palladian style. An immense lawn stretched in front of the house, only serving to further set off its grandeur. Only a hint of the large gardens Nathaniel had told her were behind the house could be seen from where they stood. The equally grand stable block could just be made out behind a copse of trees, set to one side and behind the house.

Nathaniel was blithering on about it, blissfully oblivious to Kitty's despair. To him this was simply home. He had known no other way of living and could not imagine anyone finding it intimidating.

Kitty's silence finally broke through to him as he wound his lengthy spiel down.

"Do you not like it?" he asked worriedly.

"No, no. It is lovely," she hastened to reassure him. "Very elegant." She hesitated before admitting what was really bothering her. "It is just so *huge*."

Nathaniel looked back down at the sprawling home laid before them and tried to see it through her eyes. It *did* have the longest façade in all of England. And there *were* over three hundred rooms. And the stables *did* accommodate over one hundred horses, even if he did not have quite so many stabled there himself. On occasion, house guests *had* even be known to get lost inside and require a guide to find their bedchambers.

He was a little chagrined to realize he had failed to properly prepare his wife for her homecoming. He rushed to try to reassure her. "It is quite large, but we have a wonderful staff that care for all the day-to-day duties. I am sure Mrs. Davis, the housekeeper, will be of much help to you as you learn what is required of you as the mistress. And once my mother has returned to the dower house you will be able to apply to her for the answers to any questions you may have. No one is expecting you to take over everything right away."

Kitty did not find as much reassurance in his words as he would have liked her to, but she managed to summon a smile and a nod.

"Are you ready to go on down?" Nathaniel asked.

She responded in the affirmative and he led her back to the coach and handed her up for the short drive to the house. They were greeted by the staff at the door, all eager to meet the new mistress.

Kitty was handed out of the coach only to be met by and introduced to a dizzying array of servants. Her head spinning with names by the end of it, she desperately hoped no one expected her to be able to remember all those names right away.

Mercifully, once the introductions were over, Nathaniel led her into the house. He pointed out a few of the principal rooms as they passed them on the way to their chambers. They were both ready to shed their dusty travel clothes and refresh themselves after their long journey.

The full house and grounds tour would have to wait for another day, as the extensive property would take more time than they had to go over fully. But he was looking forward to showing her a few of the rooms where she would most likely be spending a great deal of her time.

It was quite a trek from the main entrance to the master and mistress' chambers, but Nathaniel assured Kitty that there were more convenient entrances that could be used by the family. The main entrance was generally only in use by arriving guests or on formal occasions.

Nathaniel found himself to be unexpectedly nervous as they neared his wife's new quarters. Would she approve of them? Were there enough windows for her taste? Would the furnishings suit her style? He expected her to want to make some decorating changes, and had left the room as his mother had vacated it in anticipation of Kitty's arrival.

He paused before the door briefly, with his hand on the knob, to address his wife, "These are your chambers. I hope you find them satisfactory."

Nathaniel opened the door and allowed her to precede him into the room. He followed hesitantly behind her, unsure of her reaction.

Kitty walked to the center of the room and looked all around her, taking in the overall view before inspecting further.

The four poster canopy bed was set against the hall wall, with a sofa at the foot of the bed and a small table set before it. A large fireplace took up much of the wall to the left, along with one door that led to a small sitting room and another to her dressing room beyond it. Three large windows blanketed the room with light and a small desk and chair was set against the windows to take advantage of the illumination. The wall to the right held the connecting door between their rooms, as well as a small grouping of comfortable armchairs. The high tray ceiling only served to increase the grandeur and elegance set before her.

The wallpaper was a bit faded, and there was a slight air of neglect about it that attested to its disuse, but overall the rooms were alight with an air of indisputable sophistication. There was very little Kitty would have chosen to change, except for the sake of making the rooms her own.

Nathaniel had managed to keep his silence as she explored the space, but upon her reentrance into the bedroom he could not help but ask, "Does it meet with your approval? I thought you would like to make some changes yourself so I have left it until now."

"They are lovely rooms," she commented. "I should like to change the paper and the curtains, but other than that, I find them very satisfactory."

"I am pleased you think so." He moved toward the connecting door. "I will leave you now to change and rest. Mrs. Davis has assigned you a lady's maid for the time being, but if you would prefer to choose one for yourself I am sure she can arrange for some interviews." He turned the doorknob and pulled the door open. "When you have rested, just knock on the connecting door, and I will show you around the house."

Kitty stood stock still for several seconds after Nathaniel shut the door behind himself. The reality of where that door led had not hit her until he had used it so nonchalantly. Of course, she had known that this was a typical living situation between a husband and wife. She had spent a great deal of time at Pemberley in the past year with Elizabeth, and her knowledge of such matters had grown exponentially under her newly married sister's tutelage.

But to suddenly to be thrust in the situation herself, without the love match her sisters enjoyed, was quite a different thing! She was nervous about what such easy access might mean for her relationship with Nathaniel, but took solace in their current friendship status. He was an honorable man, a true gentleman, as he had shown by marrying her under the circumstances. Surely, if he meant to take advantage, he would have done so already.

These thoughts served to calm her somewhat and she was able to answer the light knock on the hallway door with some composure.

The young lady that was admitted introduced herself as, "Fanny, ma'am. I's be the lady maid Mrs. Davis has assigned to yer."

She did not look to be much older than Kitty herself, and she found the young lady's chatter and cheerful personality to be not unlike that of her own sisters. The thought was comforting, given the distance that separated her from her family, and she cheerfully set about learning all she could about the household from Fanny, firmly pushing her apprehensions to the back of her mind as the maid helped her out of her dusty clothes.

At length, when Kitty had changed into a suitable gown and Fanny had coaxed her hair into an elegant chignon, whisking away the requisite cap with a firm, "Yer hair is much too fine to hide away under a cap, ma'am. The Master should not like it," she worked up her courage to knock on the connecting door.

Her first knock going unanswered, she grew curious, and hesitantly cracked open the door and peeked in.

The room on this side of the door was decidedly masculine. She could see her husband's touches throughout. The bed was dark and heavy, with four large posters extending to the ceiling. The other pieces of furniture were similarly massive, with dark wood and green accents. She suspected, though, that the pieces had been chosen for their comfort, rather than any fashionable purposes on her husband's part.

His six foot frame would not easily fit in the petite, delicate pieces of current fashion. In addition, as this room was unlikely to be seen by any except the most intimate of family members and the servants, he was at liberty to keep the room as he liked it instead of conforming to the fickle fashions of the Ton.

Kitty espied her husband settled deep into an armchair by the window, book in hand. He had not looked up at the creak of the door, so she could only assume that he was too absorbed in what he was reading to notice what was going on around him. She took a moment to study him, noticing his clean clothes and refreshed manner.

She called out quietly, hoping to attract his attention without having to venture further, "Nathaniel?"

It was enough. He looked up at the sound of her voice and smiled at the sight of her in the doorway.

"I knocked but you did not answer."

"Oh, right. Sorry about that. Sometimes when I start reading I tend to block everything else out." He held up the book as proof of his words and she noticed the title.

"Race horses? Are you planning on raising race horses?"

"Hmm… well yes, actually. I should rather like to get into raising them. I should not want to race them, I think; too risky. But the stables here at Cheventhorpe have room for up to one hundred horses, and a good race horse is worth quite a bit of money." He grinned widely. "Besides, you have met Abaccus. They are prodigious fun to ride."

"I imagine they are," she said, remembering their long ago conversation on the topic.

He too seemed to remember this, and quickly changed the topic to a more amicable one. He rose and set the tome aside to offer her his arm. "Should you like to see the house?"

She acquiesced and they set off to view some of the more principal rooms of the house. Her husband was a charming tour guide, telling her funny anecdotes about some the rooms, and providing her with tips on how to find her way around the massive house.

Thus the day passed, until the bell rang to signify it was time to change for dinner, at which time they parted to pursue their toilette. Fanny was very pleased with the opportunity this presented to play dress up with her already pretty mistress, and went to great lengths to present her to her best advantage.

Kitty almost did not recognize herself in the mirror when Fanny had completed her ministrations. Surely that sophisticated lady staring back at her could not be the same person as the lowly Kitty Bennet!

In a sense, she was not the same person she had been even the morning before. She was a married woman now, and a Marchioness at that. These new shoes she was to fill would take some getting used to.

She was still admiring herself at the mirror when a knock sounded from the connecting door.

"Come in!" she called out, knowing very well it was her husband.

The door slowly creaked open and Nathaniel's head popped around the corner. "Are you ready to go down for…" His voice trailed off as he got a good look at his wife. A smile slowly stretched across his face. He stepped further into the room. "Ah. Yes, I see you are." He bowed dramatically over the hand she offered him. "You look quite exquisite."

She giggled at his theatrics and twirled so he could see the complete ensemble. "Is not the dress just lovely? It is one of the new ones I had made in London. Fanny convinced me I simply must wear it."

"Yes, it is beautiful. But not as beautiful as the woman who wears it."

Kitty blushed at the compliment and took the arm he offered her.

"Do you think you can guide us to the dining room without any help from me?" Nathaniel asked, hoping to distract himself from the vision beside him.

Her brow furrowed in concentration as she tried to picture the route in her head. Then a smile lit up her face. "I think I can, yes."

"Then lead the way, milady." Nathaniel was glad the challenge distracted her from paying attention to him, as it left him free to sneak peeks at her while they walked. It was virtually impossible not to stare at the pretty picture she presented this evening.

Just when he thought he could resign himself to being just friends, at least for the time being, she had to flaunt what he could not have. But an evening spent in her vivacious company was still far preferable to one spent alone here or at his club in Town. There was never a dull moment to be had.

Kitty smiled triumphantly as the dining room doors appeared before them.

He smiled. "Very well! What a quick study you are! You shall know your way around the whole house before long."

"I intend to," she stated confidently, and they went in to dine.

The meal that was set before them was extravagant, even by Cheventhorpe's standards. Nathaniel had the sneaking suspicion that Cook had gone to great lengths this night to make a good impression on the new mistress. There were no less than three courses served, and each of them had a selection of dishes to tempt any palate. Nathaniel was half afraid the selection would be overwhelming to his new bride, but she nonchalantly helped herself to a few of her favorite dishes and some of those new to her as well.

He was proud of her adventurous spirit as she delicately tasted some of Cook's lesser known French dishes, and a little appalled when she pointed out his more limited selections.

He hastened to assure her that he had indeed, tried those dishes not so long ago and found them not to his liking, so there was no need for him to try them again. His cook's refined tastes were no match for his preference for English fare, and the unusual dishes upon the table were a reflection of his cook's hopes that the Mistress would appreciate his exotic tastes.

It seemed that these hopes were well-founded, as at the conclusion of the meal Kate asked the butler to inform Cook of the excellence of the meal and to express her appreciation of his excellent menu. Nathaniel could only imagine the smug look that was sure to grace his cook's face upon that declaration, and prepared himself to find many foreign dishes upon his table in the future.

Nathaniel accompanied his wife into the drawing room, preferring to forgo the usual port for the pleasure of her company. He was also a little afraid she might get lost along the way if he left her to her own devices. Although she had shown considerable skill in navigating them to the dining room, the distance between the drawing room and dining room was too great to leave the matter to chance.

Kitty was pleased to have him accompany her, as this too had been a concern of hers. They settled in the warm drawing room, a fire crackling merrily in the grate and reflecting off the planes of their faces. At first, they found themselves at a loss of what to do with themselves. Kitty did not have her usual mending to occupy herself with after dinner, and Nathaniel had little experience in an evening at home spent in other than his own or his mother's company.

Eventually a game of backgammon was suggested, and taken up wholeheartedly by both parties.

When the time came for them to retire, they wound their way back through the infinite hallways to their chambers, Nathaniel leading the way, as Kitty's mind was wont to wonder in its tired state. He paused outside her door to bid her goodnight and watched her disappear inside before seeking his own rest in his chambers.

*****

The next day dawned dark and dreary, with the imminent threat of rain. Kitty was disappointed when she first pulled back the curtains to reveal the gray sky, as, in her lively nature, she had looked forward to exploring the vast estate. But there was still much to explore inside, and so with Fanny's animated chatter to encourage her, she soon set forth, ready for the day.

It did not take her long to get lost.

*****

Nathaniel appeared at breakfast fully expecting Kitty to already be there waiting on him. He had gotten caught up in some estate matters before breakfast and had somehow managed to completely lose track of time. He had almost decided to send for a tray and forget about going down himself, but had decided that it was probably not good form on his part to abandon his wife on her first morning at Cheventhorpe.

He was surprised, therefore, to find the room empty save for the lone footman installed by the door. He frowned at his wife's absence and asked the servant, "Has Lady Rockingham requested a tray this morning?"

He was assured that no, Lady Rockingham had not made such a request, and indeed none of the servants had seen hide nor hair of her since Fanny had completed her toilette that morning.

He sighed and snagged a few muffins from the buffet before he went searching, instructing his servants to inform him if they happened upon his wife.

He began his search in the part of the house closest to their quarters, thinking she would not have wandered far, and in fact had probably just gotten wrapped up in something like he had.

She was not there. He wound his way through the hallways, checking each room as he passed for a petite brunette. He had made his way to the completely other end of the house before he stumbled upon her.

He opened the door to the conservatory and peered inside, but the abundance of plants made it impossible to get an unobstructed view of the place. He went inside to search more thoroughly.

As he probed further into the conservatory he could make out the faint sound of someone humming. He turned and followed the sound, hoping it would lead him to Kate. The noise drew him nearer until finally there was a break in the greenery and he was able to see his wife, merrily snipping away at the plants with a pair of shears.

He grinned at the sight of her and leaned his shoulder against a large plant stand. "Have you forgotten about breakfast?"

She looked up at the sound of his voice and smiled warmly, but he did not miss the relief in her eyes at the sight of him. "I am afraid I got rather lost," she admitted ruefully. "After awhile all the corridors started to look the same and there was no one around to direct me. Then I stumbled on to this little piece of paradise and decided to stay put for awhile in the hopes someone would notice my absence and come find me."

"Well, I have found you now, and fortunately for you, I know my way back to the main rooms. But I am afraid you have missed breakfast in the process."

She rubbed absently at her stomach. "That is disappointing."

He laughed and pulled out his pilfered muffins. "Happily, I brought some with me to share."

Her eyes lit up.

He gestured to a small bench situated nearby. "Shall we sit down to break our fast?" They seated themselves upon it and she eagerly took the muffin he offered her and they fell to eating in a companionable silence.

When all that was left of their meal was crumbs, Nathaniel looked around him and said, "It has been ages since I have been in this part of the house."

"Really?" Kitty asked in surprise. "Why ever not? It is a beautiful place to be, especially when the weather prevents you from being outdoors, like today."

"I do not know," he admitted. "Sometimes I get so caught up in estate business and overseeing the tenants I forget there is more to Cheventhorpe than my study."

Her brow furrowed at his mention of business. "Am I keeping you from your work?"

"No. My steward is more than capable of handling anything of importance." He stood up and offered her his arm. "Today the only necessary business I have is showing my wife her new home. Shall I give you the full tour?"

She readily accepted and they set off together. He led her through the hallways, trying to help paint a mental picture for her of the floor plan of the house as they walked. The formal rooms held little interest for her, as they were rarely used, but she needed to know their location and where other rooms were located in conjunction with them. It was the personal rooms that held appeal to her.

Nathaniel paused outside one door and smiled down at her with his hand upon the knob. "This is another room I have not been inside in quite a long while."

With her curiosity peaked, she eagerly followed him inside.

"The nursery has been closed up for some time now," he commented. "My parents kept it open for a long time after I was born, hoping for more children, but it was not to be. Still, I have some fond memories of this place."

Most of the furniture had been moved to the attic and what was left had been covered with cloths to prevent fading. There was a film of dust on every surface and the air was thick with neglect. But Kitty could still imagine it as it once was, full of laughter and play. Even those years would have been few though, as the room had sunk again into disuse once Nathaniel had been sent away to school.

Nathaniel did not voice his thoughts as Kitty looked around the room, peering out the windows and running her fingers over the mantle. There was hope for this room once again, now that he had taken a wife. Perhaps, in time, their own children would play here. He could imagine the room ringing with the sounds of laughter and children's voices, the nurse trying desperately to quiet them, lest they disturb some guest or interrupt some evening's entertainment. The mental image brought a smile to his face that Kitty attributed to his fond memories. He was glad to let her continue to think so.

The next room on their stop held considerably less appeal for Nathaniel, as it was the room that had served as his own for the few and far between times he had returned from school. The transition away from home had not been an easy one and he had often resented his parents' choice to send him away.

It had taken him a long time to find his niche at school and begin to feel as if he fit in there. He had made a few close friends and some good memories during those years that he still cherished, but he was never so happy as to the completion of his education and the opportunity now afforded to him to return home for good and begin learning the managing of the estate.

Unfortunately, the time under his father's tutelage had been all too short. Only six months after his return his father had taken ill, never to recover. The management of the estate had fallen on his ill-prepared shoulders and he had struggled in the ensuing months to learn to balance his responsibilities. It had taken him awhile, but he felt that he had finally come into his own as Master of Cheventhorpe.

He was proud of what he had accomplished. He had brought Cheventhorpe to even further profitability, doubling its production from its time under his father's hands. Now he hoped to add to its notoriety and profit by adding race horses to his assets.

Racing itself was too risky a business for his blood, but there were a great many out there, including the Prince himself, that fancied the sport and spent a great deal of money acquiring a fleet of race horses. His own love of horseflesh had only served to sweeten the deal.

They spent very little time in that room, as Nathaniel remained silent on the subject, and Kitty found the room to hold little of interest. It was void, empty of life, with nothing in it to reflect the boy her husband had once been.

They quickly moved on and spent an enjoyable day exploring the house and reliving Nathaniel's old memories until Nathaniel was called away by his steward to attend to some matters shortly before dinner.

Kitty could hardly fault him for this, despite his regret for having to leave her to her own devices. She settled herself instead in the little sitting room attached to her own chambers with some embroidery and sought to wile away the time until she could reasonably change for dinner.

*****

The next morning found her in a meeting with the housekeeper before breakfast was served. By the time she emerged, her head was spinning with all the details involved in running the large household. Thankfully, she found Mrs. Davis had it all under control, and there was very little really required of her at that time other than a few necessary decisions on the menu to be made. A good staff really was invaluable. But those meetings were to become a part of her daily life.

She met Nathaniel at breakfast. She entered to find him already seated at the table, a cup of coffee in hand and the newspaper open before him. She filled her own plate and sat down beside him with a sigh.

He looked up at the noise and smiled warmly at her. "Now what has you so down already this morning?"

She fiddled with the food before her. "I have just come from my first meeting with Mrs. Davis."

He smiled knowingly. "Ah. That is an occasion to cause one some apprehension. But the perks of the job outweigh the responsibilities, I think you will find." His smile took on a mischievous edge. "And to prove my point, I have a surprise planned for after breakfast."

She cocked her head, her interest peaked. "Really? What is it?"

He laughed. "You will not find out that easy. Eat your breakfast. You will know soon enough."

Breakfast did not last long after that. Soon, he was leading her out of the house towards the stables. Her excitement grew as they neared. She remembered a conversation from the very beginning of their acquaintance and tried to keep her hopes in check as they walked.

It was only a short distance from the house to the stables. Kitty was impressed with how well-kept the stalls were and how well-maintained the building was. Nathaniel led her down the row of stalls, past the carriage horses and hunters, only to pause outside one particular stall door. He bade Kitty to look inside.

As she did so, he explained, "This is Luna. She is very sweet and docile. Never thrown anyone in her life. I have kept her for my mother mainly, but as she rarely deigns to ride anymore, I thought you might like to use her. I have remembered, you see, that you like to ride but have lacked the opportunity."

Kitty was silent as she inspected the mare before her. She was delicate and friendly, approaching Kitty was a light whicker to gently snuffle the hand she held out to her. Her black coat had been brushed until she shone, and her long mane and tail had been carefully groomed. But Kitty could not help but feel a twinge of disappointment.

This horse, as lovely as she was, would present no challenge for her. Despite of her lack of opportunity, she was proud of the horsewoman she was and resented the implication the sweet-tempered horse represented.

Nathaniel grew nervous at her silence. "Should you like to give her a go?"

Kitty swallowed her pride. At least she would have the opportunity now to pursue the sport she so enjoyed, even if it was not on a Thoroughbred like Abaccus. "I should like to very much."

A wide smile broke out upon Nathaniel's face in relief at her answer. "I will have them saddle Abaccus and Luna while we change into riding clothes."

A short while later they were changed and on horseback. Nathaniel led the way as they set off into the surrounding hills. Abaccus was frisky and raring for a good run. Nathaniel had a hard time trying to keep him under control. Kitty had no such problems with her placid mare, who was perfectly content to plod along at her own slow pace.

Nathaniel was finally forced to admit defeat. He told Kitty, "I have to let him work off some steam before he will settle down. If you want to keep riding in this direction, I will let him have a good run and then come find you in ten minutes or so."

Kitty readily acquiesced, thinking she might have some time to put the little mare through her own, admittedly lesser, paces while Nathaniel was busy elsewhere.

He cantered off to enjoy his gallop and she took a few minutes to study her surroundings before a slow smile broke across her face and she set off to the east.

The source of her delight was a low wall set about a clearing. Probably originally intended to keep cattle or sheep in, the pasture it surrounded was currently empty. She scouted around the wall, looking for any safety hazards, before she withdrew to get a running start.

She managed to get the tame mare up to a canter before neatly jumping the wall. The little horse seemed shocked that so much was being asked of her, but she gamely responded to Kitty's direction with her best. Kitty leaned down to pat the mare on the neck. "Good girl," she murmured. She turned her around to hop back over the wall and see if she could get her up to a fast canter on the other side. Kitty regretted the necessity of the unstable sidesaddle, for it prevented her from galloping freely the way she would have like to.

Luna begrudgingly got up to speed for her and Kitty relaxed at the feel of the wind in her face. She was free, flying under the power of the animal beneath her. It was exhilarating to let loose from the constrains of society and to be at peace with the world around her. There was nothing so natural for her as being on horseback.

She let out a sigh of relief to once again be in the saddle. It was like coming home. She reined her horse in as the sound of another rider approaching broke through her reverie, and by the time Nathaniel broke into view she was moving at a sedate trot. Luna seemed to be pleased to return to a civilized pace, but Kitty could not help but be disappointed. Her moment of independence had been all too brief.

Nathaniel eyed her suspiciously as he neared. She appeared to be riding at the modest pace expected of a gentlewoman, but her appearance suggested otherwise. Her bonnet was dangling down her back by its strings. Tangled strands of her hair had come loose from her neat up-do and fallen to frame her face. Her cheeks were pink from exertion. But she had traveled no farther than he would have expected her to at an easy trot.

He dismissed his suppositions as unlikely, given her inexperience with horses, and decided a strong gust of wind must have done the damage to her appearance.

"Are you enjoying your ride?" he asked instead.

"Very much so," she said as a guilty blush stole over her cheeks. She asked hastily, "How was your run?"

"Wonderful. Abaccus is a very smooth mover. Hopefully, now that he has worked out some of his energy he will behave himself like a proper gentleman."

They set off over the fields. Quite awhile later, they returned to the house and saw their mounts into the capable hands of their grooms.

The first week of their marriage passed by in a similar fashion. Every morning before breakfast, Nathaniel would care for his correspondence and any necessary business and Kitty would meet with Mrs. Davis. They would break their fast together, then Kitty would go for a ride on Luna and Nathaniel would accompany her if he did not have any pressing matters to care for. After that, they would go their separate ways, not to meet again until dinner. Their evenings were spent in close company, normally with some game to hold their attention, but occasionally with only their conversation to entertain.

Kitty was gradually becoming acquainted with the layout of the great house and had only managed to become slightly lost one more time as she had tried to return to the conservatory. She had been able to sort that out after a few well-calculated turns, and had emerged victoriously from the opposite end of the house.

They had made some progress, she felt, in their professed friendship. The time spent in close proximity facilitated this. Kitty felt herself to be settling into married life and could only be glad that things had turned out so well under the circumstances.

Nathaniel was not as satisfied as she. For, while her fears had turned out to be unfounded, his hopes had not yet been fully realized. He was happy that there was no animosity between them, yet he was discontent with the extent of their relationship. Patience was not a strong suit of his, and he struggled with the necessity of biding his time. Only time could heal all things between them and help their budding affection grow into something more substantial and lasting.

Ten days after their wedding, Lady Cecelia returned to Cheventhorpe, having given the newlyweds some time to find their footing as a couple. She took up residence in the dower house, only a short ride or drive away from the main residence.

Kitty was eager to see the lady who had so set her at ease again, and set off the morning after her arrival home under the pretense of inviting her to dine at Cheventhorpe that evening.

Kitty was unaware of the clear line of sight that the upper levels of the dower house had of Cheventhorpe and the lands between, and so took the opportunity once she was out of sight of the main house to push the little mare to her limits.

Lady Cecelia watched her approach from one of the upper windows with a smile. Her son had certainly found himself an unconventional bride. This was no simpering miss. The confident woman on horseback bore no resemblance to the hesitant young lady who had seemed so out of her element in London.

While no horsewoman herself, Cecelia could recognize the elegant carriage and fine seat Kitty exhibited. As she neared the house and slowed her pace, her control over the animal was exemplary. It was easy to see what her son had missed. She needed a mount more equal to her talents. Her frustration with the little mare's limits was obvious.

Cecelia moved away from the window as Kitty made the turn on to the drive. It would not do to be caught staring at the window.

She was seated to her advantage on a little sofa by the window when Kitty was shown in. She rose eagerly to meet her daughter-in-law with an embrace. She bid her to sit beside her.

"Tell me, how do you find Cheventhorpe? Are you settling in?" Cecelia asked.

"It is a lovely estate. I was a bit overwhelmed at first. It is just so terribly daunting, you see. But Mrs. Davis has been of a great help to me with my household duties, and I think I am managing tolerably well. I have not been lost above twice and even then I discovered some very pretty parts of the house, so it was not so terribly bad."

"And how has my son been treating you? I know he can easily get caught up in estate affairs to the exclusion of all else."

Kitty blushed at the mention of Nathaniel and answered slowly, "I think he is putting forth effort to help me feel welcome. He makes it a point to have breakfast together and discuss our plans for the day. He tries to join me on my ride afterwards whenever he is able."

Cecelia was satisfied with this answer, at least for the moment, and went on to question her further on her accommodations in the house. This set the stage for an enjoyable chat, at the end of which Kitty left well-pleased with herself, having secured Cecelia's acceptance of the dinner invitation.

*****

That evening found Kitty fretting over the menu and dinner arrangements. Fanny had to keep reminding her to hold still as she tried to coax her unruly waves into submission. The maid's frustration was tangible, hanging in the air like a fog in the room. Kitty felt guilty for adding to her problems and resolved not to fidget. But her mind still rolled with all the things that could go wrong at that night's dinner.

She desperately wanted things to go off without a hitch. This was her opportunity to prove to her mother-in-law and husband that she was worthy of the title that had been bestowed upon her. It was also a trial run for any future dinner engagements that were sure to come. How things went tonight would give her a good idea whether she was ready to begin entertaining their neighbors.

Fanny had just helped her into her gown when a knock sounded at the connecting door. The maid ran an appraising eye over her and nodded in satisfaction before retreating out the hall door.

"Come in!" Kitty called as the door closed behind Fanny. She moved to collect her shawl from the bed.

Nathaniel popped his head around the door and, noticing that her back was turned to him, came a few steps into the room. "Are you ready to go down? Mother should be here within half an hour."

"Just a moment," she murmured distractedly, now searching for a wayward slipper. He was treated to a nice view as she bent over to look under the bed. He averted his eyes quickly as she rose victorious, holding up the errant shoe. "Here it is!" She slipped it on her one bare foot, revealing a nicely turned ankle.

He had to clear his throat to be able to force out the words stuck there. "Congratulations. Now we can go down." His tone was unintentionally sarcastic as he struggled to rein in his roving thoughts.

The smile faded from Kitty's face at his manner, but he was too distracted to notice. They descended the stairs and took up waiting in the drawing room. Kitty sat in tense silence wondering what she had done wrong, while Nathaniel paced near the window, trying to keep his mind off his lovely wife, oblivious to her discomfort.

When Cecelia arrived she immediately noticed Kitty's downcast countenance and her son's distraction. Her mouth thinned as her eyes flew from one to the other. She sized up the situation in a moment, deducing accurately that Nathaniel must have done something to alienate his wife.

She greeted Kitty warmly, putting a grateful smile back on the younger woman's face with her easy affection. Her son received a far cooler welcome, along with a look he remembered from his childhood that conveyed her displeasure and disappointment in him.

Nathaniel was startled to be on the receiving end of that glare. What on earth had he done to warrant that? She had only been in the house for a few moments! There had not even been enough time to do anything to offend her.

Dinner was ready before there was time for much more discussion, so Nathaniel offered each lady an arm and they went in to dine. They were silent as they waited for the servants to set out the first course and clear the room.

"How did you find London, Mother?" Nathaniel asked his mother politely, hoping the conversation would eventually lead to whatever he had done.

He underestimated her. Cecelia's conversation was light and unaffected as she related a humorous tale from her time in Town. She was clearly able to hold her own counsel until she was ready to divulge her thoughts. His frustration and confusion grew as she continued speaking.

The story achieved her purpose in telling it. A smile returned to Kitty's face, and whatever had been bothering her was pushed to the back of her mind. She even laughed lightly at one point in the story.

Her goal complete, Cecelia easily steered the conversation in a new direction as the second course was brought in. "I noticed you rode over this morning on Luna, Catherine. How do you find her? I myself was never much of a horsewoman, but I know you enjoy the sport."

Kitty carefully worded her reply. It would not do to appear ungrateful for the gift, even if she was a bit bored with the mare. "She has a very gentle nature."

Cecelia waved the words away with her fork. "By which you mean she is rather boring. Nathaniel would say the same thing if he was forced to ride such a dull creature."

Kitty laughed at her outspokenness even as Nathaniel bridled at her words.

"Now see here..." he started.

He was interrupted by his mother. "It is perfectly true Nathaniel. *I* do not mind a mount with so little initiative, but Catherine needs a horse with more spirit."

He scowled at her words but made no further disagreement. Cecelia was content with that. She had planted the idea in his head. With time he would realize the truth of the matter and be compelled do something about it.

Kitty glanced between the two of them, uncomfortable with the tension between her husband and his mother. She was not about to deny that she found Luna to be uninteresting, but she did not want to be the cause of dissension in the family either, especially as she was now part of that family!

"It is fortunate that you have such a spirited mount for yourself in Abaccus," she ventured. "Were you able to find time to exercise him today since you were unable to accompany me on my ride?"

Nathaniel shook his head. "No. I shall have to rely on the grooms to make sure he was exercised."

Kitty cocked her head. "Can your grooms handle him?"

He grinned wryly. "A few of them can, if only barely. It is a good test to see if they are ready to handle racehorses."

"I should think so."

They set down their utensils as the servants returned to remove the second course and lay out the third and final course. The conversation drifted into Nathaniel's plans for the future of Cheventhorpe as they lingered over their dessert.

Eventually though, the ladies rose and left Nathaniel to his port, withdrawing to the parlor. He swirled the liquid in his glass and watched as it lapped at the sides. Was he really so blind as to miss his wife's abilities on horseback? It was true, he had assumed that lacking the opportunities he had, she would naturally need a more docile mount. But he had to admit to himself that he had not really paid any attention to how good a horsewoman she really was. He was always so consumed with his own ride he failed to take any note of hers.

He resolved to be more diligent in watching her in the saddle. If there was truth to his mother's words, then he needed to consider the next steps he would take. He took a sip from his glass and leaned back in his seat. But that still did not explain what had caused his mother to be so offended earlier.

*****

"That was a delightful dinner, Catherine," Cecelia complimented her as they sipped their tea. "The dishes were excellent and the white soup extraordinary."

"I am glad it pleased you," she demurred. "I simply followed Mrs. Davis' suggestions."

"A wise choice. A great lady understands the value of delegation. You will have no problems entertaining the neighborhood."

"I appreciate your confidence, although I cannot share it. I fear my education was not what it should be for a lady."

"Nonsense." Cecelia waved away her concerns. "That is rubbish. You will learn far more about the real duties of a lady having been thrust into the role than you would under a governess in any gentleman's home."

"Still, I should have liked to feel more prepared."

"That, I grant you, is valid. We should all like to be prepared for what life throws our way. But that is rarely the case, as I have found. We can only do the best we can with what we have."

Kitty's eyes twinkled. "Fortunately for me then, my resources are more abundant than formerly."

Cecelia laughed. "I should think so."

Nathaniel came upon them at that moment, and they both looked up at his entrance, laughter in their eyes. It warmed his heart to see the two most important women in his life clearly enjoying each other's company. The evening passed with pleasant conversation, but Nathaniel did not easily forget his mother's censure, and nor did she.

At the conclusion of the evening, when her carriage had been called for and was at the door, she requested, "Walk me to my carriage please, Nathaniel."

He gladly obliged, recognizing that here, at last, was a chance to clear the air. They were silent along the way, but Cecelia stilled him with a hand on his arm as he made to hand her into the carriage.

"I know not what occurred here before my arrival," she began. "But I do know that the first thing I noticed upon my arrival is that you were completely ignoring your wife, and she was very downcast. Now, I have done what I can to lighten her mood, but young women can be very fragile sometimes, Nathaniel. I would caution you to take care with your manners toward her. Your words can do much good, but they can also do much harm." She gave him a motherly kiss on the cheek and alighted into her carriage. "Congratulate Catherine on the meal tonight. She will do you proud as Lady Rockingham."

He retreated a few steps to watch as her carriage gradually disappeared into the night. He had much to think about as he made his way slowly inside.

He repeated her words in his mind and replayed the evening's events. He admitted with a sigh that his mother was right. His earlier words to Kate in her room had come out clipped and cold, even though it was far from intentional. He would have to focus on not allowing her beauty to affect him so.

As if that were possible.

CHAPTER SEVEN

Kitty was woken earlier than usual a couple days later by Fanny bustling about her room, stoking the fire and refilling the washbasin. She rubbed sleepy eyes and rose up on her elbows to inquire of the maid, "Whatever is all the fuss about?"

Fanny dropped a curtsey. "Begging your pardon, ma'am, but it's sure it is that it's going to be a busy day for ya, and you'll be wantin' to get an early start." She resumed her activity, this time pulling back the curtains to let in the bright morning light.

Kitty groaned at the harsh light and fell back on her pillows. "Why ever would today be any different than any other day?"

"Because Lady Rockingham- pardon me, the Dowager Lady Rockingham- has returned. All the neighbors be takin' that as a sign that ya be ready to receive callers."

Kitty sat straight back up in bed. "You are joking."

Fanny looked confused. "No ma'am. Why's would I do that? Tuesday be the customary day for Cheventhorpe to receive visitors. All the servants be abuzz with talk of it.

Sarah, one of the kitchen maids, her sister be a maid for Mrs. Milbank and she done sent word the missus be eager to meet the new Lady Rockingham today."

Kitty groaned. She was not in the least ready to receive the local gentry. She had only just managed to be able to find her own way around the maze of hallways.

"You's best be getting up now ma'am if ya are wanting to be looking your best for your company," Fanny advised.

Kitty sighed and dragged herself out of her warm, comfortable bed. "You are right, of course."

Next door, Nathaniel was already awake and almost completely dressed by the time the commotion arose in his wife's room. The first rays of morning light always served to awaken him, and his valet was used to his habits. He preferred to get as much done by breakfast as he could so he was free to ride with Kate.

He could just make out the rise and fall of Kate's voice along with the interspersed comments of what he assumed was her maid. The sound of her voice through the thin wall made him smile. She did not sound very happy.

He allowed his valet to finishing tying his cravat and shrugged on his coat before dismissing the man. He meandered near the connecting door, and still hearing slightly raised voices, he knocked gently on it. Receiving no answer, he cracked the door and let himself in.

"I say, Kate, is everything all ri…" The words died on his lips.

He had caught her in her undress. She blushed furiously and wrapped her dressing gown around her as far as she could make it stretch. He felt the tips of his own ears go hot at the sight of her standing before him in her nightgown.

She could barely look at him in her embarrassment, but forced herself to answer him, "Everything is fine, Nathaniel."

He cleared his throat. "Well, then.." His voice trailed off as he stared at his wife, but he somehow managed to gather his wits back about him. "I suppose I shall leave you two to carry on then." He retreated back behind the closed door.

On her side of the door, the sight of Fanny's knowing grin irked Kitty. "Do you not have something you ought to be doing?"

For his part, Nathaniel leaned back against the closed door as a slow smile spread across his face. What a way to start the morning! He stepped away from the wall, whistling a jaunty tune, and went to find his steward to start the morning's work.

*****

They met again over the breakfast table. Kitty had managed to compose herself in the intervening time. She knew she looked very well, as Fanny had gone to great lengths to ensure she looked her best for company. Her gown was lilac, to bring out her green eyes, and her hair was swept up stylishly. She was the picture of an elegant lady, exactly as she imagined a marchioness should look. Only this knowledge had given her the confidence she needed to face her husband after that disastrous morning.

Nathaniel took in her appearance with approval and slight disappointment. She would do him proud in front of the visitors they were bound to receive that morning. But strangely, he found he preferred Kate as she had been this morning, disheveled and sleepy-eyed in her nightgown, with a braid thrown over one shoulder, to the sophisticated woman before him now.

It was his first real glimpse of the free-spirited woman he had met at the beginning of their acquaintance since they had returned to Cheventhorpe. She had kept herself under careful regulation as she tried to fit into her new role as mistress. But he could not help but miss her carefree attitude.

"I see you are prepared for visitors today," he commented.

"Yes. Fanny was so kind as to inform me of the likelihood." She spoke calmly, but he could see her anxiety and irritation simmering under the surface.

"I am sure you shall have no trouble entertaining them. The local gentry are nosy, to be sure, but they are kind-hearted. They will truly only wish you well."

Kitty nodded, appreciating the words as the encouragement they were meant to be, but inwardly acknowledging the little they did to dissuade her apprehension.

"Perhaps, when the visiting hours are over, you and I can take a ride before dinner." Nathaniel watched her carefully to gauge her reaction to the suggestion.

She brightened at his offer, having been loath to give up the joy of her daily ride for the rigors of the drawing room. "I should like that very much."

They separated soon after that; she to await their visitors in the drawing room, and he to peruse the ledgers with his steward in the study.

The first arrivals were shown in not half an hour later. As Fanny had predicted, Kitty soon learned that her guests were no other than Mrs. Milbank and her four daughters, Blanche, Moriah, Mabel, and Phoebe. The girls ranged in age from the eldest, Blanche, at nineteen, to the youngest, Phoebe, at sixteen, one year apart all down the line. When the pleasantries were out of the way, Kitty found herself heartedly thankful for her unusual upbringing.

The decibel level soon grew to unheard of heights as Mrs. Milbank and her daughters all tried to speak over each other and vie for Kitty's attention. If she was anyone else, Kitty's head would have been spinning from the noise. Instead, a small smile began to work its way across her face at their resemblance to her own family.

They were perhaps not the most elegant family, but, as Nathaniel had said, they were goodhearted. As the visit neared its end, Kitty could not help but be disappointed by their quick departure.

She did not have long to wax nostalgic, as her next visitors arrived soon after.

So it went, until Kitty felt she had received all of Yorkshire in her drawing room.

Nathaniel could not help but be distracted by the thought of Kate down the hall entertaining their neighbors. His thoughts consumed him, completely pushing any business matters out of his mind, as he wondered how she was faring, if she was overwhelmed or dealing confidently with whatever was thrown at her. He finally had to dismiss his steward, as he could tell the other man was growing frustrated with his distraction.

Instead he paced by the window, watching as the carriages came and went. When the hours allotted to receiving visitors had concluded and the last carriage had faded in the distance, he hurried down the hallway to see how Kate had fared.

The door to the drawing room was open and he paused in the doorway just to drink in the sight of her. She stood at the window overlooking the drive, her back to him. She looked just as elegant and composed as she had at the breakfast table that morning.

He leaned his shoulder against the door frame. "Did it go well then?"

She turned with a smile at the sound of his voice. "It did."

"Are you ready for our ride?"

Her smile grew. "I am."

*****

Nathaniel could see Kate visibly relax as the stables faded in the distance behind them. He watched her from the corner of his eyes as a slight smile turned up the corners of her mouth, but her expert handling of her mount eventually drew his attention.

On a whim, one part of his mind toying with the notion of seeing how she handled the challenge, he suggested, "How about a race?"

She looked up at him, startled briefly, before a grin stretched over her face. She pointed out, "It would hardly be fair. Abaccus would easily outdistance us."

"I will give you a head sta- Hey!" He laughed as she spurred the little mare as fast as she could safely go before the words were even out of his mouth.

He held Abaccus back, as the stallion was eager to pursue, and watched how his wife urged Luna on. His heart sank as he remembered his mother's words. She was right. Kate needed a different horse, one that could match her spirited personality.

He let Abaccus have his head and they started to close the distance. As they drew nearer Kate looked back over her shoulder at them and urged her horse even faster. Nathaniel was surprised at the sudden burst of speed, as he did not think the little mare had any more to give.

As he drew abreast of Kate, he realized that she was laughing. Pure, free, unrestrained laughter. It startled him, the joy upon her face. But it made his heart sing to see her that way. This was how he wanted her always to be with him, unadulterated and unrestrained, living in the moment.

With a few more strides, Abaccus easily overtook her, and they both gradually slowed their horses. She was still laughing at the thrill of the ride and the sense of pure freedom it gave her as he dismounted and came around to help her down.

She slid down into his arms, her head thrown back and her eyes shining. "That was magnificent!"

Nathaniel could not find the words to respond. She was breath-taking. She had lost her hat somehow and the wind had torn her hair loose from its pins. It cascaded in waves down her back and billowed around her face. Her face was flushed with excitement and her eyes shone like emeralds with joy. *This* was how she should be. *This* was the carefree spirit that had first attracted him. *This* was his wife. Not the controlled persona at the breakfast table that morning.

But it was her lips that caught and held his attention. He could not help but lean closer as the laughter died on her lips and the air between them thickened with tension. Her lips parted slightly in anticipation as he lowered his head until they were only a hair's breadth apart. He could almost taste her on his lips.

Abaccus' insistent whinny startled them both. They jumped apart as if they were schoolchildren, found out by the headmistress. Kitty ducked her head and moved away, her cheeks pink with embarrassment. How easily she had forgotten her resolve!

Nathaniel silently berated himself as he picked up the loose reins of their horses and tied them to a nearby tree branch. It was too soon to allow himself to indulge in such pleasures! They were not yet ready to pursue what that could only lead to. But when she was like this, tousled and free, his reasonable mind simply stopped working. She was different than any woman he had ever met. He could not seem to resist her allure, no matter how hard he tried.

He was fortunate to have secured her hand in marriage before some other young fellow had stumbled upon her, hidden away in the countryside of Hertfordshire.

He returned from tying their horses to find Kitty had taken up a seat on a nearby rock. He flopped down on the ground next to her, heedless of the damage the wet grass might do to his clothes. Neither of them made eye contact. Kitty picked absently at a loose thread on her habit while Nathaniel plucked at the wet grass around him.

Their thoughts followed similar paths. Kitty's mind roiled with emotion. She had *wanted* him to kiss her. When his gaze had settled on her mouth her lips had tingled in anticipation. She had acted with all the impetuousness of a schoolgirl with her first crush, instead of the reasoning of a grown woman considering her future. Indeed, she had acted no better than Lydia had with Wickham!

The attraction between them was undeniable. She certainly could feel it, and it was evident he also felt its magnetic pull. But there had to be *more* than that if they were to pursue a true husband and wife relationship. She could not give herself wholly to a man without loving him and knowing she was loved in return.

They were both hesitant to break the silence between them, neither knowing how to tell the other what they were feeling nor how to approach such a subject.

It was Nathaniel who finally spoke. He stood and held his hand out to help her up. "We had better return to the house to change for dinner."

*****

When they met over the breakfast table the next morning, Nathaniel had an unusual question to ask of his wife.

"Do you know how to ride astride?" he asked.

Kitty was so startled by the abrupt question that she nearly dropped her toast in her tea. The impropriety of what he suggested made her face burn as she admitted guiltily, "I do."

Nathaniel pondered her answer as he chewed his eggs. She had expected condemnation or, at the very least, shock.

But he seemed unaffected by her admission and maybe a little...*pleased*.

His next statement made her forget about her breakfast all together.

"I want you to ride Abaccus when we go out this morning."

Her jaw dropped. "What?"

"I want you to ride Abaccus. I want to see if you are capable of handling him."

Her heart pounded at the prospect. To have the opportunity to handle such a magnificent mount?! It was beyond her wildest imaginations.

Before she could make any reply he continued, "I have one condition though. I want you to ride astride. Mrs. Davis should be able to find you an old pair of short pants somewhere to wear. Abaccus is far too skittish and he is not broke for sidesaddle. I will not take the chance of him throwing you when you could have far more stability and control astride."

Kitty was too flummoxed to do anything but nod her assent.

*****

She felt positively ridiculous as Fanny helped her into an old pair of Nathaniel's short pants after breakfast. Although they must have been *at least* ten years out of fashion and had obviously been made for her husband before he hit a growth spurt, they were still far too large for her petite frame.

They had appropriated a pair of suspenders from Nathaniel's wardrobe to hold them up, but there was still a large gap between her small waist and the waist of the pants. Fanny fretted over this detail for several minutes before inspiration struck.

The maid rummaged through Kitty's things until she found a suitably worn length of ribbon. "Just you hold on a minute, my lady, and we'll have ya fixed up in a jiffy." She tacked on the ribbon to the waistband of the pants with a few well-placed stitches, leaving the two ends dangling free. "There now, ma'am, we'll just tie these two ends tight, and there ya be!"

Kitty was impressed with her solution, as hastily done as it may have been. It might not look impressive, but it certainly did the job. Still, the image that greeted her in the mirror was far from elegant.

The short pants ballooned out from her waist to her knees, like two swollen pickles. Kitty sighed. An unfortunate choice in color, that. She was a sight to behold. But she was not about to let that stop her from riding Abaccus, no matter how the servants and Nathaniel might laugh.

She kept her head held high as she made her way through the hallways, ignoring the looks she got along the way. Nathaniel struggled not to grin at the ridiculous picture she painted as she greeted him in the stable yard. He had not thought how she would look in his short pants when he had suggested the idea, but it was certainly better done in theory than reality. She moved regally toward him, her eyes defying him to laugh at her.

It was apparent they had been waiting for her to arrive. He stood at the head of a black stallion she had never seen him ride before, while a groom held Abaccus for her. They brought out a mounting block and she swung easily up and into the saddle, gathering the reins in her hands.

Nathaniel made sure she was settled and had Abaccus firmly in hand before he mounted his own horse and led the way out of the yard.

They rode at a restrained pace for some time before Nathaniel suggested a gallop. Both their animals were chomping at the bit to stretch their legs, and he was convinced by now that Kate would be able to handle the challenge, even astride his willful mount.

When they reined their horses in sometime later to a more reasonable speed, he was convinced that he had underestimated his wife. She kept Abaccus firmly in check and her seat and handling were impeccable. In some ways she was a better rider than he.

By the time they returned their mounts to the stables, he knew a trip to Town was in order. He told her as much over the dinner table.

Her voice and face went carefully neutral. "Do you mean to leave me here?"

He looked up from his plate in confusion. "I shall not be gone above three or four days on business. There is no need for you to accompany me. I thought you should prefer to stay here."

She swallowed hard to force down the panic that threaten to choke her. On her own, here at Cheventhorpe? Not even a fortnight since she had first arrived? Was her husband to abandon her so soon? She managed to answer coolly, "Very well then. I see you are not to be dissuaded."

He was not a man used to including others in his decision-making and so took this as an indication of her agreement and brought up the subject no more. But such was not the case. She was hurt at his exclusion of herself and such blatant disregard for her opinion on the matter. How far they still had to go in communicating openly with one another!

She retired early that night, claiming a headache. Nathaniel was disappointed to be deprived so of her company, especially considering the early start of his journey the next morning. It was unlikely she would wake early enough to see him off and he had hoped for an evening of easy camaraderie to remember while he was in Town.

He retired soon after, claiming the excuse of an early morning, but finding the parlor to lose its appeal without the presence of his wife. Even the pages of a good book failed to distract him that night.

They both laid awake in bed, unable to find sleep, with only a thin wall standing between them physically, but a myriad misunderstandings separating them emotionally.

Kitty was still awake when Nathaniel rose the next morning. The gray light of dawn was just beginning to filter over the horizon and break through a crack in the curtains. She rose and pulled her dressing gown around herself as noise from his chambers reached her. She strained her ears to identify every sound. That splash would be him washing up. Next, that scraping would be him shaving. The low murmuring was probably him discussing the day's clothing with his valet.

She longed to go to him and tell him how she really felt- that she despaired of how she would get on by herself; that his presence here was what made her feel at home. But she could not. Stubborn pride stayed her feet whenever they strayed too close to the door that stood between them.

Eventually she heard the hall door open and close, and the noises coming from the other side of the wall ceased. She moved to the window, pulling back the curtains to afford herself a view of the drive. It was not long before he appeared below, taking Abaccus' reins from the groom and swinging easily in the saddle.

She was strangely numb inside as she watched him ride away, growing smaller and smaller in the distance. Her heart fluttered once in her chest as he paused at the top of the hill to turn back for a final look at the house, but it was but a moment and then he was gone.

Kitty felt the pinpricks of tears forming at the back of her eyes and wiped them away disgustedly. She was not so weak as this! It was good he had gone. Now she would see what she was really made of. She turned away from the window and firmly shoved the curtains back together.

When she finally appeared below stairs, she had made up her mind. Passing the butler in the hall on the way to breakfast, she ordered the carriage to be brought round for her in an hour's time. The butler inquired, ever so politely, as to her destination.

"I mean to call on the Milbanks of course. It is only proper that I should return their visit."

"Rightly so, ma'am." He bowed and removed himself to see to her request.

She was slightly miffed at his questioning, but knew she was only transferring her irritation at Nathaniel to the servants. She had best watch her tongue today lest she lash out at some poor unsuspecting person.

The breakfast room was lonely that morning. She had never realized how the huge room echoed with the absence of any human voices. She ate her meal in silence, nothing but the clinking of her silverware and coffee cup to keep her company.

She was glad to escape the empty rooms when the appointed time for the carriage to be brought round arrived. The clatter of the horses' hooves on the drive and the snap of the reins were a welcome relief from the house's oppressive silence.

It was not a far drive to the Milbank's home, once they cleared Cheventhorpe's own property. Kitty tried to enjoy the pleasant scenery and note the directions as they traveled in an attempt to calm her racing heart. There was no reason to be nervous, she reminded herself. This family was achingly like her own. They would be delighted to receive her.

Still, she had to tamp down her nerves as she climbed the front stairs and was shown into the parlor. Immediately upon entering though, she was put at ease.

All five Milbank ladies were present and they all rose with squeals of delight as she was announced. She was veritably thronged by the women as they vied over who she should sit next to. Their enthusiasm brought a smile to her face. It was nice to be so sought after. She had rarely felt so in her own family home, and even here at Cheventhorpe Nathaniel still sometimes made her feel unwanted. Like when he had left her here so callously.

She pushed those unwanted thoughts to the back of her mind and focused instead on the positive reception. She was not going to let negative memories ruin this day for her.

She took a deep breath and asked after the neighborhood, a question she knew would have been irresistible for her own mother.

The Milbanks were more than willing to fill her in on the local news, often speaking over each other and in ever-increasing tones. Kitty smiled calmly and responded as she could, at ease in the chaotic environment.

They were reaching the conclusion of the visit when Miss Mabel spoke up, "Is it true, Lady Rockingham, that you mean to have a dinner party?"

"A dinner party?" Kitty said, a little shocked and taken aback. The very idea was overwhelming. She tried to conceal her panic behind a composed veneer.

"Oh, do hold a dinner party!" Miss Phoebe squealed abruptly.

Miss Milbank smiled serenely and added reasonably, "It would be an excellent way to meet new friends."

Kitty could not deny this to be true, and knew full well that if she was ever to truly fit in with the local society she would have to expand her company beyond that of her husband and mother-in-law. She agreed hesitantly, "Very well. Shall we name a date then?"

They settled on the Tuesday next, and Kitty departed for her next destination with the anticipation of plans to be made. At least now she had something with which to fill her time while Nathaniel was away.

She arrived home after her round of the neighborhood, exhausted but pleased with her excursion. She felt she had truly fulfilled her role as Lady Rockingham and she was quite proud of herself.

Coming home was a cruel reminder of her own insignificance. She went almost immediately up to change for dinner, and then sat down in all her opulence to dine… by herself.

The servants paraded in to set out the first course, and then out again, leaving Kitty with the table stretching infinitely before her and the room echoing forlornly with the clink of her silverware. She was dwarfed by the massive empty room and felt instantly the ridiculousness of her position there. She belonged in the intimate quarters of Longbourn, where the rooms did not outshine her with their magnificence.

She was thoroughly disheartened by the end of the third course and immediately retired to her rooms. The plans for her dinner party would have to wait for her morning meeting with Mrs. Davis, so there was nothing to distract her from her thoughts.

The connecting door taunted her from across the room. Fanny was waiting to help her prepare for bed, but she dismissed her as soon as she was out of her gown. A lifetime of sharing a maid with a household of sisters meant she was more than able to care for her own toilette.

She seated herself in front of her dressing table and set about taking out all the pins Fanny had used to tame her curls, for the benefit of whom, she did not know. She might as well have taken a tray in her room and eaten in her nightgown.

When all the pins were out and her locks were down around her shoulders, she began the tedious process of brushing out the tangles her unruly curls created. She cringed as the brush caught on a particularly rough snarl.

She finished her toilette and climbed into bed, leaving one candle burning on the nightstand to dispel the sudden hostility of the large room. She laid in bed for a long time, watching the flickering shadows cast on the wall by the lone flame.

It was Nathaniel's warm presence that had made the huge house feel like home. Without him, the thick walls were only an empty shell that threatened to swallow her up within their embrace. She felt acutely her aloneness. For all her newfound wealth and seeming security, this life was nothing without someone to share it with.

She smiled grimly in the near darkness. Her mother would be horrified if she were privy to her thoughts. She had everything that her mother, in her limited understanding, could ever comprehend anyone desiring- money, carriages, clothes, even a title. But it was not enough. Her mind admitted ruefully to itself what she most deeply desired, and yet could not have: the love of her husband.

She revolted at the thought of *that word* and pushed those thoughts to the back of her mind. Still, her heart cried his name fervently.

Nathaniel.

Where was he on this dark, moonless night? Was he safe and warm in bed, sleeping dreamlessly? Was he thinking of her, as she was of him?

She could not know. Her heart ached with loneliness and yearning. The connecting door mocked her from its place within the shadows, taunting her with the lack of his presence, tempting her with his memory.

She rose slowly from her bed and wrapped her dressing gown tightly around herself. She picked up the lone candle in its holder and braved the shadows to stand in front of the door, bathing it in the flickering light.

She stood there for some moments, hesitant and unsure, her gaze on the glimmering knob. She finally gathered her courage and placed her hand on the knob, turning it slowly and feeling the door give way under the pressure of her hand.

It swung open and she took two hesitant steps forward to cross the threshold. The light from her candle illuminated only the few feet surrounding her, but she could make out the silhouettes of his furniture.

Her feet carried her across the room to the large bed and into it before she was consciously aware that it was her destination. She took a deep breath as she settled into the plush pillows and felt a small smile grace her lips. It smelled of him- spice and leather and something that was uniquely Nathaniel. She pulled a pillow closer, hugging it against her chest and burying her nose in it.

Surrounded by his scent, Kitty drifted off to sleep, her candle flickering weakly, forgotten on the nightstand.

CHAPTER EIGHT

Kitty woke the next morning disoriented. The gray light that filtered through a crack in the heavy curtains revealed that it was early morning- far earlier than she was used to rising. Her internal clock was off after foregoing her usual evening entertainment for the allure of bed.

Groggily, she pulled herself up out of the plush mattress into a sitting position and wiped her eyes. It took her several moments to make the connection between her masculine surroundings and her late night wanderings. When she did, she flushed scarlet and glanced down at the pillow she still clutched. She quickly set it aside.

In the light of day, her loneliness seemed juvenile and petty. She was embarrassed to be so weak. At least no one had been privy to her switch, and hopefully it would stay that way. She reluctantly climbed out of the warm bed and pulled her dressing gown around her. She shivered in the cool morning air, the maids not having been in to light the fires yet.

Quickly, she made up the bed, leaving it exactly as she had found it, and hurried back to her own room. She closed the door firmly behind her, forgetting her candlestick where it had burnt out beside the bed.

*****

Fanny found her snuggled deep under her own covers sometime later. The maid came in and threw open the curtains to let the light in. She turned and laughed at the sight of a pair of eyes barely peeping out at her from under the down bedding.

"It's a right crisp mornin' we be having, my Lady. Ya just stay under those covers until I get this here fire a-going."

Kitty was more than happy to do as she suggested. She returned to reading the book she had stowed under the covers until the room gradually warmed to a more comfortable temperature.

She emerged from the bedding and stepped into the dressing gown Fanny held out for her. She took a seat at the vanity while Fanny disappeared into her dressing room to pull out a morning gown.

With no one but the servants to appreciate her clothing choice, she rejected the more elaborate gown Fanny picked out for a far simpler one she had often worn at home. The disgruntled maid muttered under her breath the whole time she was helping Kitty into it, but Kitty could not help but smile at herself in the mirror.

This was the woman she knew. She was not pretending to be someone she was not or trying to live up to anyone's expectations. She was just plain, ordinary Kitty.

She instructed Fanny to pull her hair back simply and departed soon after for her morning meeting with Mrs. Davis.

She had much to discuss with that lady about her planned dinner party and they spent some time together, going over the details and working up a menu.

When she finally appeared in the breakfast room awhile later, her stomach was complaining of her neglect. So hungry was she, that she barely noticed the emptiness of the room and the loneliness of eating by herself.

Instead, she concentrated on filling her stomach while her mind went over her plans for the day. She had every intention of treating herself to a nice long ride after breakfast. Then, she had the invitations for her dinner party to write and send. Surely, that would fill the majority of her day. If not, then she could work on some embroidery, or read a book. She would find some way to fill her days until Nathaniel returned.

When her plate was empty, she rose and ascended to her chambers to change for her ride. Soon enough, she found herself on horseback, leaving behind the confines of Cheventhorpe. She passed out of sight of the house and urged Luna into a canter, reveling in the joy she felt with the wind in her face. No sooner, though, had she reined in her mount than that feeling of freedom faded. She guided Luna to a small stream nearby and dismounted, letting her graze with her reins looped over a low-hanging branch.

Kitty seated herself on a large stone near the water's edge and sighed. She was frustrated with her inability to distract herself and frustrated with her riotous emotions. One moment she was resolute and resolved in her determination, the next she was wavering and lax. She was thoroughly tired of her own insecurities and inabilities. She longed for Lizzy's firm, almost stubborn ways, or even Lydia's carelessness. Perhaps if she did not care so much she should be able to go on like it was any other day.

Even Jane's calm, endearing disposition should have been a welcome change from this wishy-washiness she suffered from. Mary's ability to lose herself in a book or the pianoforte was also something to be wished for. Nothing could distract her right now, not even one of her favorite activities.

Her pent up dissatisfaction sought a release. She stood and picked up the nearest object at hand, which happened to be a small rock. Grasping it firmly, she summoned all the vehemence and anger she felt and hurled it with all her strength into the shrubbery across the stream. The thud it caused as it hit the ground filled her with satisfaction. She continued her rampage, sending stones and branches careening and heaving into the woods and water, each one fueling her zeal.

She shouted in triumph and threw her hands up in the air at the loud thwack one rather large stone made as it crashed into a tree trunk. The sound of her voice startled a pair of partridges in the nearby brush, sending them scattering from the shrubbery, and startling Kitty in the process.

She jumped at their abrupt appearance and then laughed at herself.

"Go there, you silly birds!" she shouted after them, still laughing. "Leave me be!"

She twirled from her place atop the rock and laughed hysterically until tears poured down her cheeks. Finally, she collapsed back on the rock and buried her face in her hands, groaning at the ridiculous portrait she painted, yet oddly at peace with herself, her anger spent.

She stayed that way for some time until a large nose nudged her and she looked up into the worried eyes of Luna, standing over her. She laughed at the mare's expression and reached up to catch the reins dangling from her bridle and pat her on the muzzle.

"It is all right, girl," she hastened to reassure her. "I am fine."

The mare bobbed her head, as if to agree, and then looked in the direction of the house, pulling gently on the reins, as if to say it was time they headed home.

"I can take the hint," Kitty said with a smile. "I guess we have been gone long enough." She led the mare to a nearby fallen log and mounted, turning her in the direction of home. The little mare was only too happy to oblige.

When they arrived back at the house, Kitty found they had been gone far longer than she had anticipated. She would have to hurry to write her invitations if she wished them to go with the next post. She fell to doing so with urgency, taking care to keep her handwriting elegant and legible. She was pleased with the result when she sat back to look them over, and happily placed them in the tray to be sent out.

She was ensconced in her sitting room sometime later with some handkerchiefs to embroider, when a footman appeared in the doorway.

"An express for you, my Lady," he intoned, and held out the missive to her.

She took it and thanked him. He disappeared from sight as she curiously inspected the address. The handwriting was unfamiliar to her, and she cracked the seal, taking in a sharp breath as she recognized the signature.

Nathaniel Watson, Marquess of Rockingham.

It was really a rather short note, simply informing her of his safe arrival, of his hope to return the following day, but of the likelihood his business would extend an extra day.

Unbeknownst to her, he had waffled for some time over how to address the note. He did not wish to appear too overly formal and yet at the same time he could not appear too intimate. In the end, he had simply addressed it *My Dear Kate*, and concluded it *Yours*, and hoped she should not think it too overly familiar of him.

Kitty's heart fluttered a little at the greeting and conclusion, and a rosy flush colored her cheeks. But the emotions that welled at the words were not unpleasant, and in fact, she was quite gratified by the supposition that perhaps there was some real feeling between them. She read the note twice more, looking for any other hint of preference in the formal wording, but found none.

She folded it up as the hour for dinner approached and Fanny came to help her dress, leaving it out beside her bed for further perusal.

She ate her meal hurriedly, eager to escape the confines of the room for the more pleasant space of her own chambers. She retired early again, impatiently allowing Fanny to help her into her nightclothes.

As soon as the maid had left the room, she opened the connecting door and scrambled into Nathaniel's bed, taking the letter with her. She reread his words, hearing his voice in her head, surrounded by his most intimate possessions. She could almost feel his presence here. Her heart still missed his company, but it was consoled by his note. She fell asleep easily, still grasping his letter tightly in her hand.

*****

The next day passed in much the same way as the day before. Kitty went for a ride, worked on some embroidery, read a book, and was disappointed when her husband's hoped-for return did not occur. She climbed into his bed for the third night in a row and woke the next morning with the happy knowledge that today he would be home.

With this is mind, she allowed Fanny to pick out a more elaborate morning dress than she had worn the last few mornings, and to spend extra time styling her hair into an elegant fashion.

She purposefully stayed close to home, foregoing her normal ride after breakfast for some embroidery in the parlor, where she could watch the drive and listen for any approaching riders.

Alas, her diligence was not to be rewarded until late in the day, just before she was to go up and change for dinner. She was tidying up the drawing room and putting away her embroidery when a commotion outside drew her attention.

She crossed to the window and peered out. Her heart skipped a beat at the sight of Nathaniel below, dismounted and speaking with one of the grooms. How had she missed him riding up the drive?

She would have to hurry if she wanted to catch him before he made it up to his chambers to change out of his dusty traveling clothes. She hastened out of the room, only pausing briefly to check her appearance in a mirror and reassure herself she looked well enough to greet her husband.

Her steps slowed as she neared the entrance hall. Sudden doubts surfaced in her mind. Her palms turned clammy with nerves. How would he receive her? What if he was not as glad to see her as she was to see him?

She need not have worried. She stepped hesitantly into the entrance hall just as he was handing off his hat and gloves to a footman. He turned his head at the sound of her footsteps and grinned widely at her appearance.

"Good evening, Kate." He closed the distance between them and took her cold hands within his. "You look well."

She inclined her head and said, "Good evening, Nathaniel. Did you have a good trip?" The words came out stiffer than she had meant them to as she battled her uncertainty.

His wide smile belied any nervousness on her part as he tucked her hand in his arm and led the way to their chambers. "I did. I was able to accomplish what I needed to. I am very glad to be home though."

"I am glad you have returned safely, also," Kitty admitted shyly. "I was rather bored while you were gone. But I do have some news to tell you."

Nathaniel's smile only widened at her admission. It was good to be missed. Surely that was a sign of the growing affection between them?

"What news do you have?" he asked.

She proceeded to fill him in on her plans for their dinner party. While surprised at all she had accomplished during his absence, he was pleased to see her taking the initiative and stepping into her role. He questioned her lightly as they walked, abstracting tidbits of her activities in the last few days. He was reluctant to part as they approached their separate rooms.

The last few days without her company had been tiring and incessant. To be once again in her vibrant presence was a gift, one he would never take for granted again. He felt whole with her at his side, in a way he had not realized he had been missing until they were reunited. He wanted to hear every detail of her days without him and listen to the lilt of her voice as she spoke. He wanted to make her laugh and see her on the back of a horse with the wind in her hair.

But he recognized the necessity of a separation for the time being, and reluctantly left her at her door to enter his own. A familiar, yet unidentifiable scent floated in the air, barely perceptible, but enough to give him pause as he entered. His brow furrowed, he sniffed, trying to a catch a whiff of the light scent.

Lemons, he thought. And something else. Something unique. His smile widened as he identified it and his gaze flew to the connecting door and the low hum of voices that filtered to him through the wall. He closed the door behind him and went to change out of his traveling clothes into something more presentable.

He reemerged from his dressing room awhile later, freshly washed and shaven, in clean clothes and feeling infinitely more refreshed. He caught a glimpse of something out of place from the corner of his eye as he passed the bed and turned his head to seek it out, frowning.

His gaze softened as it alighted on the burned-out candlestick on his bedside table. The nub of misshapen wax and the blackened wick provided proof of his suspicions. As one piece of the puzzle fell into place, he looked around him for further clues. Looking closely, he noticed the slightly rumpled bedding and that his pillow was a little further to the left than usual. As he lingered near the bed he caught a whiff of the same unique scent, the one he knew belonged solely to Kate. He took a step towards the bed and the scent strengthened.

He picked up the misplaced pillow and held it up to his nose, drawing in a deep breath. It was unmistakable. He ran a lingering hand over the wrinkled bed clothes and a soft smile graced his lips as he connected the dots.

His wife had been in his bed.

The knowledge was strangely intimate. It lit a hope within him that her heart was opening towards him in the same way his was slowly but surely being drawn to her.

He could not know her thoughts or reasons for seeking his bed, and he dared not ask. Her attempts to cover up her meanderings were enough to convince him that she wanted them to remain private. But he could imagine and suppose, and that supposition brought with it hope.

His heart filled with a sweet warmth, he crossed the room to knock on the connecting door and collect his wife for dinner.

*****

Tuesday dawned clear and bright, and brought with it a flurry of activity. Kitty forewent her usual after-breakfast ride to oversee the preparations for her dinner party.

Nathaniel was disappointed by her absence, as he had come to view that time fondly as *their* time and was loath to trade such pleasantries for his study. But he was also glad to have his wife so otherwise distracted as he was expecting a very special delivery that morning that he did not want her to see quite yet.

He spent several long hours in the privacy of his study, listening to the servants bustle through the halls and trying to concentrate on his ledgers before his butler appeared in the doorway.

"My Lord, the delivery you were expecting has arrived," he intoned solemnly.

Nathaniel brightened. "Very good! Is my wife occupied?"

"She is presently with Mrs. Davis, going over the dinner menu."

"Very well." He rose and went outside to see about his delivery, secure in the knowledge that his wife was otherwise engaged.

*****

Nathaniel is in an inexplicably good mood, Kitty thought. She could hear him humming happily to himself through the wall as she sat patiently waiting for Fanny to arrange her hair.

She had barely seen him all day, as wrapped up as she had been in her plans and preparations. The hectic day had served to keep her nerves at bay, with no time to think about anything going wrong. But now the butterflies in her stomach kicked up as she sat idly.

She felt a flash of irritation at her husband as a particularly loud and jubilant note carried through the wall. What was just another dinner party to him was a momentous occasion for her. Did he not realize what tonight meant?

Here was her chance to prove herself. The local society would be judging her, seeing whether she was a fit mistress for Cheventhorpe. All the gossip the next day would dwell on her- on the hostess she had or had not been. So much could go wrong yet. How could he take it so lightly?

Fanny only chuckled at Nathaniel's exuberance. "I be thinking the master be right looking forward to tonight. And right he be too. I never seen no lady as pretty as you are going to look tonight."

Kitty smiled tightly. "That is because you have never been far from Cheventhorpe, Fanny. If you had, you would realize there are many ladies far more beautiful and accomplished than I am."

Fanny paused and patted her on the shoulder. "Now, my Lady, you may think that, but the Master sure don't feel that way. I never seen a gent look as fondly at a lady like he does at you."

Kitty took her words with a grain of salt. Fanny had only her best interests at heart, and while what she said was obviously wishful thinking, she had only meant to reassure. She could not know how things really stood between Nathaniel and Kitty.

She chose to ignore the comment and redirect the conversation. "I was thinking the purple silk for tonight."

Fanny eagerly took up the topic and soon they were in a lively debate over gown choices. In the end, Kitty's original suggestion reigned, and Fanny helped her slip into the deep eggplant dress. She looked in the mirror, pleased with her reflection. The selection of colors available to her as a married woman opened up a whole new wardrobe. The richer jewel tones played up her light green eyes and complimented her complexion. Her skin glowed in the light and her eyes shone brilliantly.

The string of pearls that Fanny had woven through her elaborate hairstyle glistened, winking merrily as they caught the candlelight and dodged in and out of her rich chestnut locks. Tonight she wore her hair half up and half down.

She had made concession to her youth and refused to wear the more matronly fashions that many would have expected of her now, as a married lady. She might be the Marchioness of Rockingham, but she was still young. She wanted to feel like herself tonight. To be Kitty. She could not do that hiding behind someone else's expectations of how she should look and dress.

A knock came at the connecting door as Fanny was fastening a simple gold necklace around her throat.

"Come in!" she called out, recognizing her husband's distinctive knock. He entered confidently at the sound of her voice and took a seat on the sofa at the end of the bed as Fanny put the final touches on her ensemble. Nathaniel's eyes gleamed with appreciation as he took in her appearance.

Fanny smiled triumphantly at his appraising look and waggled her eyebrows at Kitty as if to say, "I told you so."

Kitty raised one eyebrow and shook her head slightly at the other young woman in exasperation. "Thank you, Fanny. You may go now."

Fanny curtseyed and let herself out, only pausing briefly in the doorway to cast one last self-satisfied smirk over her shoulder at Kitty. Nathaniel raised one eyebrow at the interchange between his wife and her maid but chose not to comment.

Instead, he rose from his seat and came to take his wife's hands. "You look absolutely magnificent tonight. I shall be very jealous to have to share your company with so many."

Kitty blushed prettily. "Why, thank you, my Lord." She glanced up at him coyly from under the heavy fringe of her lashes. "You look rather well tonight as well."

Nathaniel grinned broadly at her compliment and squeezed her hands. "Are you ready for tonight?"

She grimaced at the reminder. "As much as I ever will be."

He smiled reassuringly. "You will do fine. Mrs. Davis has everything well in hand, and the neighbors will not be able to help themselves from falling for your charming ways." He lifted her hands to place a gentle kiss on each of her palms. "Just like I have been unable to."

Her breath hitched in her chest as the implications of his words hit her. What could he possibly mean by that?

She did not have time to dwell on it. Nathaniel tucked one hand on his arm as if the words he had just uttered were nothing out of the ordinary and led her from her rooms. It was time for them to descend and welcome their guests.

CHAPTER NINE

By the time they went into dinner, Kitty had relaxed somewhat. Everyone that had been invited had been able to attend. For the first time, the dining room did not seem so overbearing. Kitty happily listened to the lyrical rise and fall of voices as her guests conversed around the table. She took a sip of the white soup and was pleased with Cook's efforts. Everything was going exactly to plan. She shared a smile with her husband, who had been confident in her abilities all along. He was relieved to see her finally relaxing.

One of the Misses Milbank drew her attention with a question, and she was transported back again to her own family dinners. The company of the Misses Milbank, normally so comforting to her, instead struck a bittersweet cord in her heart.

As she watched their animated faces and familial teasing, her heart yearned for her own family, especially her sisters. Jane and Elizabeth would be so proud of her tonight. Mary, although she might disapprove of the frivolity, would have jumped at the chance to perform at the pianoforte. And Lydia, poor, misguided Lydia, would have been flirting with every gentleman in the room and drinking way too much wine.

Mamma would have been on the prowl for a husband for Mary among the wealthy landowners around the table. Pappa would have been leaning back in his chair, listening to the conversations going on around him, his eyes twinkling with amusement at some joke only he understood.

She had been so caught up in all the new experiences and settling into her role as Lady Rockingham that she had not had time to miss them. But now, as she sat, the longing blossomed within her, unfurling its cruel wings in her heart. An ache settled deep in the pit of her stomach, and she swallowed hard, pressing it down as it threatened to overwhelm her.

Nathaniel looked up at that moment and happened to catch her eye. He started at the stark forlornness that he saw in her eyes. In the next moment she had managed to veil her thoughts, but he had already seen it. What had happened? Only a few minutes before she had seemed to be relaxed and content. Now her smile was forced and strained.

There was no way he would be able to pull the truth from her in a dining room full of people. He would have to bide his time until he could speak with her alone. He made a mental note to do just that before they retired for the night.

Kitty managed to keep her composure through the rest of dinner and the entertainment afterwards, but the strain was beginning to show by the time they saw their last guest off. She wanted nothing more than to take to her bed and have a good cry, thinking its cleansing powers would do her good.

She was uncharacteristically silent as she followed Nathaniel upstairs. He kept sneaking glances at her out of the corner of his eye as they climbed the stairs, but he could not seem to find the right words to bring up her change in emotions.

He left her reluctantly at her door, chastising himself for his ineptitude, and retreated to his own room.

Kitty allowed Fanny to help her undress and shrug into her nightdress, holding back the emotions that threatened to overwhelm her until she could be alone. Her maid did not seem to pick up on her obvious distress, chattering away obliviously about the evening's success and the different gowns the ladies had worn.

She was glad when she could finally dismiss her for the evening. She collapsed on her bed and allowed all the emotions she had been fighting to surge to the surface and engulf her. She could no more fight it than she could a riptide pulling her out to sea.

The tears came hot and fast, carving their path down the planes of her face. She could not summon the effort it took to wipe them away, letting them pool on her pillow in despair.

*****

On the other side of the wall, likewise ready for bed, his valet long ago dismissed, Nathaniel paced back and forth in front of their connecting door, wrestling with himself.

He knew he should go to his wife and find out what was really going on. It was his place as her husband to do so. But he balked at the connotations it brought. Were they really to such an intimate point? Or would she throw him out of the room for daring to think he deserved an explanation?

Gentleman that he was, he could not silence his conscience on the matter, regardless of how he wished to. He turned to face the door, squared his shoulders, and approached it determinedly. He knocked once on the wood, the sound reverberating in the silent room.

Nothing. There was no answer. He frowned and stepped closer, one hand raised to knock again, when he grew aware of the muffled sounds drifting through the door. He paused and leaned closer to listen.

It sounded like… crying. Instantly he was flooded with compassion and remorse. His heart ached for her and whatever it was that had caused this. Had he said or done something that might have triggered her sobs? Guilt blossomed in his gut, nagging his conscience as it sought to make its presence known.

If he was the cause, then he must make amends. He put his hand to the knob and turned it slowly, easing himself around the edge of the door.

Kitty did not notice his entrance. Her back to the door, she was too lost in her own thoughts to pay attention.

He closed the door softly behind himself and crossed to her side. His feet carried him forward of their own volition. He could no more stop himself from going to her than he could stop the sun from rising. Kitty felt the bed shift under his weight, and then gentle hands were turning her to face him.

"Kate?" he asked tenderly, pushing the hair out of her face and tucking it behind her ears. "What is wrong, my dear?" He swiped his thumbs across her cheeks, wiping away a few errant tears.

A sob caught in her throat and he gathered her close, tucking her face in the hollow of his shoulder and wrapping her in his arms. Kitty's heart thudded at his appearance, and softened at his endearment. There was more to this man she had married than met the eye. His warmth enveloped her, and she could not help but lean into him and accept the comfort he offered her.

For a long time, Nathaniel just held her, whispering sweet nothings in her ear, until finally Kitty began to tell him what was the matter. At first, he struggled to understand as she stuttered from one thought to the next, speaking almost nonsensically, but eventually he was able to draw the truth from her with a few insightful questions and concentrated effort.

He held her tighter when he finally understood what the real problem was. He could not replace her sisters in her heart. And as an only child, he could only imagine how the separation affected her. But he did understand how the dinner that night, with the overeager Milbanks in attendance, would remind her of all that she had left behind when she had become his wife.

He hurt for her, knowing full well that there was little he could do to assuage her pain. Instead, he simply held her as her sobs lessened in intensity and gradually faded away. Soon, her body relaxed into his as she slipped into slumber and he gave in to his own drooping eyelids and drifted off to sleep, still cradling her in his arms.

*****

Nathaniel woke with a start the next morning, feeling disoriented. He glanced around him, trying to place himself. Slowly, still in a sleep-induced haze, he remembered last night's events. He looked down at the peacefully sleeping form of the woman tucked against his side and his gaze softened.

His arm tingled with pins and needles under his wife's weight. There was a crick in his neck from where his head had rested against the headboard all night long. But none of that mattered.

All that mattered was the woman he held in his arms. He could still make out the traces of tears on her cheeks, but her lips were curved gently upward into a soft smile. A lock of hair fell across her cheek where it had come undone from her braid. His fingers itched to brush it back and tuck it behind her ear, but he restrained himself, reluctant to interrupt her peaceful slumber.

It felt right to wake up beside her; to have her countenance be the first thing he saw in the morning. He was complete, whole, when he held her. For the first time, he could see a fore gleam of what their future held.

What had started with attraction, and had grown to affection, had now planted the seeds of love. His mind balked at the word, claiming their limited acquaintance and rocky beginning. But his heart acknowledged what his mind rejected.

He loved his wife. There was no other reality.

It did not matter that he had only known her for a few months. He had simply been biding his time until she came into his life. There could be no other for him. He was surprised it had taken him this long to realize it.

He was under no illusions that she returned his feelings. If anything, the prior evening's display of emotion proved just how little he had replaced in her heart the family she had left behind.

But that could change, with time and effort on his part. He would woo his wife.

That tantalizing curl that refused to be held tame by her braid wafted faintly as she breathed, tickling her cheek. She stirred slightly in her sleep at its touch and he held his breath, waiting for her eyes to open. When they did not and her breathing evened again, he stretched cautious fingers and gently, carefully, tucked the lock behind her ear.

His fingers caressed her skin in its place of their own accord, and she turned her cheek and pressed it into his palm in response to the tender touch. His breath caught and held as a smile flitted across her lips, but yet she slumbered on.

He smiled. Apparently Kate was a very deep sleeper. There were so many things he still did not know about her. But he was looking forward to the learning process.

*****

It was quite some time later that Kitty finally stirred. Nathaniel felt her rousing; her breathing quickened, her eyelids fluttered, and one long limb stretched languorously, brushing against his own.

She started at the contact with his leg. Her whole body stilled, and he could sense her puzzling over it. Slowly, she opened sleepy eyes and met his gaze.

He smiled down at her tenderly and brushed that same errant lock back from where it had sprung against her cheek when she shifted. Confusion clouded her eyes.

"Nathaniel?"

"Good morning, Kate."

"Good morning." Her confusion quickly gave way to embarrassment as the fog cleared from her mind and she recalled the events of the night before. Her discomfiture only increased as she realized the compromising position she was in. Her face heated and her cheeks flushed as she struggled to sit up and put space between them.

Nathaniel was reluctant to let her go. He immediately missed the heat of her skin against his and the soft contours of her body as they molded against his side. His arms felt empty without her in them.

Kitty scooted away from Nathaniel, only stopping when her back came to stop against the headboard. She was mortified her husband had thought her so weak as to necessitate his comfort. But more so, she was ashamed to realize the pleasure she had taken in his company and the consolation he had supplied.

Nathaniel could not know the direction her thoughts had taken, but he did recognize the chagrin readily displayed on her features, and sympathized enough to seek to distract her.

"I have a surprise for you after breakfast."

It worked. She cocked her head and leaned forward, towards him. "You do? What is it?"

He laughed. "It would not be a surprise if I told you now, would it?"

She wrinkled her nose distastefully at his response, making him grin.

"It arrived yesterday while you were busy running the household ragged preparing for your dinner party," he teased.

Kitty pretended to be affronted. "I did no such thing!"

"No. I am sure they were all pleased to put their skills to use, especially Mrs. Davis."

A quiet knock at the door went unheeded as they bantered. Fanny opened the door and poked her head around the corner, surprised to hear voices as she came to stir the fire and wake her mistress. She grinned broadly upon seeing them sitting on the bed, smiling and chatting, looking for all the world like a happy couple. Well, if that weren't just about the prettiest sight she had ever seen. Pay no mind to what those gossiping biddies in the kitchen spread. The lord and lady might not know it yet, but they were made for each other. Just needed a little more time, that's all. Those two were two peas in a pod. She hummed a cheerful tune under her breath as she threw a log on the fire.

Nathaniel had noticed her entrance with a quick glance up, as he was facing the door. But Kitty did not detect Fanny's presence until the thud of the log on the fire startled her. She jumped, earning her a laughing grin from Nathaniel, and turned around.

"Fanny! I did not realize you had come in." She placed one hand on her chest to still her racing heart.

Fanny looked up from her place near the fireplace. "No my lady, I dinna think you did." She dusted off her hands and stood up. "Breakfast be served an hour later this mornin' due to ya late night. But ya be wantin' to rise soon so's ya don't miss it."

"Thank you, Fanny. You are right," Kate acknowledged. "If you would please pull out the green muslin for me, I will be ready to dress in just a moment."

Fanny curtsied and disappeared into the dressing room.

Kitty turned to Nathaniel and pulled her dressing gown a little tighter around her. She smiled weakly. "I guess I will see you at breakfast."

Nathaniel found it difficult to pull himself away from her, as necessary as he knew it to be. He wished they could have stayed that way forever, locked away in their chambers just enjoying each other's company. Instead, he pushed himself away from the headboard and climbed out of bed.

"I will see you shortly," he said from the partially open doorway. He paused before going through to add, a twinkle in his eye, "Oh, and you should probably have Fanny pull out those short pants again, because I have a feeling you are going to need them soon." Then he shut the door behind himself.

A frown creased her forehead as the door latched. Was he going to have her ride Abaccus again? She was not looking forward to making a fool of herself once more in those hideous short pants. Whatever his surprise was, it had better be worth it.

*****

The short time left before breakfast passed quickly, and it was not long after that Kitty found herself back above stairs changing into the abhorred short pants.

She might not have minded their necessity if she had known the reasons behind his request. But as it was, she hated to appear before her husband looking anything other than the lady she was striving so hard to be.

Nathaniel met her outside her chamber door just as she was preparing to go down. He was pleased with the success of his arrangements. All was in place. He had only to make her acquainted with them.

He tucked her hand around his arm and led her below stairs and out into the stable yard. Her eye immediately noted the presence of Abaccus, tossing his head impatiently, but her eye was drawn to his companion.

A beautiful, lithe Thoroughbred mare stood off to one side, her chestnut coat gleaming in the sunlight. Her muscles rippled under her coat and her luxurious tail flicked at an annoying fly as she shifted under the groom's hand.

Kitty let go of her husband's arm and went forward to greet the new addition. "Oh, Nathaniel! She is beautiful! Was this the urgent errand that took you to town?" She ran her hand reverentially over the mare's silken muzzle and brushed back her forelock.

Nathaniel was content to stand back and watch. "Is she not? Her name is Hera. I did so hope you would like her. It is a rare opportunity to find such a lovely example of horseflesh. I could not turn down the chance when I found she was for sale. You will forgive me, I hope, for rushing off so."

This statement by necessity had to be reaffirmed by many exclamations of admiration and appreciation for the animal on Kitty's part. She could not help but be awed by the magnificent creature.

At length, after much fawning, she asked, "Do you plan to breed her? Is she to be the start of your horse line?"

Nathaniel eyes widened, startled, as she obviously had mistaken his intention in bringing her out to the mare. He hastened to reassure her, "No, no! She is for you!"

Kitty's hand paused in stroking the mare's neck and she looked up, twin lines between her brows. "Pardon me?"

"I bought her for you. My mother was correct in asserting that you needed a different mount. Luna is no challenge for you. You need an animal more suited to your abilities. So I have bought Hera for you."

"For me?" Kitty still seemed dumbfounded.

Nathaniel smiled at her incomprehension. "Yes. For you."

Her brain finally seemed to compute this information. Her eyes lit with delight. Giddily, she flew to his side, crushing him momentarily with a hug and bestowing a chaste kiss on his cheek before she was back to the mare.

Nathaniel could not help but grin at her salute. He could feel her kiss still, branded on his cheek, lingering on his skin. He resisted the urge to touch the spot her lips had caressed. "Shall we go for a ride?"

This suggestion was of course immediately taken up, and very shortly they were mounted and off. They had no clear destination in mind, only an inclination to ride.

Nathaniel allowed Kate to set the pace, as she had a new mount to contend with. The mare was headstrong, but easily persuaded with Kitty in the saddle. She gave her just enough of a fight to keep things interesting, without giving Nathaniel any cause to fear for his wife's safety.

They started out slow, but Nathaniel knew Kate would want to test the mare's stamina and speed before the day was out. It was not in her nature to proceed cautiously on horseback. He pointed them in the direction of a large field that was bordered by one of his tenants, thinking to check on the man while he was in the vicinity.

He knew his wife well, it seemed. It was only a short while later that she began to test her limits, urging the mare into a trot, and then a canter, down the lane. He was content to follow her lead and match his pace to hers. She slowed as the ride lengthened and cast a sidelong glance his way. He knew from the sparkle in her eye she was eager to push the mare to her full potential.

He broke the silence that had drifted between them as Kate concentrated on controlling her mount. "There is a field just a little further on that I thought would do well for a long gallop."

Her broad grin was all the thanks he needed. She returned her attention to her mare as Hera eyed the bushes on the side of the lane and tried to sneak her head out for a bite.

Kitty kicked Hera into a canter as the long-awaited field came into view a little while later. She threw Nathaniel a mischievous smile over her shoulder and called back, "Catch me if you can!"

He was more than happy to oblige, his laughter ringing out in the open field as he gave Abaccus his head. The stallion leapt into pursuit, eager to regain the lead. But the distance between the two riders was more difficult to eat up than either of them had expected.

He could feel Abaccus' confusion as they failed to gain enough ground to overtake Hera and Kitty before they ran out of field. But the realization could not damper Nathaniel's spirits. He was proud of how well-matched the two mounts were, and how perfectly Hera suited his wife. He had chosen well.

He reined up beside Kitty at the low wall that separated the field from his tenant's land. She wore a triumphant smile at his approach and quickly began bragging of her victory.

Nathaniel contorted his face into a mock scowl, but he could not fully hide his joy in her pleasure. "You cheated! I would hardly call that a victory."

Her eyes sparkled with mirth. "Then you must challenge me to a real race sometime."

He grinned. "Perhaps I shall."

Kitty sobered as their eyes met and held. She held one hand out to him, bridging the space between their mounts, and he savored her soft touch as he took it in his own. "She is perfect, Nathaniel. Thank you."

Nathaniel swallowed back the emotions that threatened to spill over at the soft light in her eyes and answered rather stiffly. "I am pleased you approve." He released her hand and turned his horse toward the wall gate, leaning down to unlatch it.

"Where are you going?" Kitty called after him, frowning.

"I have a tenant that lives just over the next rise. I thought to call on him while we were here. Are you not coming along?"

Kitty was at once horror-stricken. "You want me to appear before one of your tenants like this?"

Nathaniel turned to glance over his shoulder at her. It was true that their romp through the field had left her curls disheveled and spilling down her back, and she could only look ridiculous in his short pants. But she was never so beautiful to him as she was on horseback. Any man would see the prize he had won in her hand, regardless of the state of her attire, and no tenant of his would ever dare to question or remark on the appearance of the mistress of Cheventhorpe.

He shrugged and turned back to go through the gate. "You look well enough. Come along now."

Disgruntled, Kitty could do nothing but follow him through the gate and over the rise, mumbling under her breath all the while at the follies of men.

When they crested the knoll, the sight of a tidy cottage and yard greeted them. Kitty was pleased to see how well-maintained it was and was reassured by the evidence of her husband's generous care in the accommodations for his tenants.

Several small children playing in the dusty yard noticed their approach and ran inside, presumably to summon their mother. Sure enough, shortly thereafter a haggard looking young woman appeared in the door way, small faces peeping out from behind her skirts.

A tired smile lit her face as they drew nearer and she recognized Nathaniel. "Good morning, my Lord," she called.

A young boy of perhaps around ten years of age appeared from around the corner of the house and held their horses' bridles as Nathaniel and Kitty dismounted. Kitty stood self-consciously to the side and a little behind Nathaniel as he introduced her to the young mother and then inquired as to her husband. Finding that the man was in the fields for the day, he proceeded to engage her in conversation on the state of the home and other matters.

Her eyes wandering as the other two talked, Kitty noted that the current fashion could not hide that the woman was heavy with child. She could only have a few more weeks before the babe was due. Looking around, she quickly counted five more little heads, all stair-stepped in age and size. The youngest could not be two, and the eldest would be the lad standing at their mounts' heads.

It was no wonder the woman looked exhausted! Kitty felt pity for the young mother, a Mrs. Robinson. She could only be five or six years older than Kitty herself. She needed a chance to rest and get off her feet, especially with five little ones and no servant to do the difficult work.

Kitty was brought back to the present as Nathaniel wrapped up his conversation with Mrs. Robinson. She said all that was polite and required of her in conclusion and then allowed her husband to help her back into the saddle. Her mind was working furiously as they rode away from the little cottage and back towards home.

She felt almost guilty as they made their way back to the massive halls of Cheventhorpe. For one to have so much and another to have so little… It was not quite right. She had been fortunate in her circumstances indeed, if not quite as happily so as some of her sisters.

She hazarded a glance at her husband as they climbed the stairs to their chambers. To marry a man she hardly knew… she had been very fortunate indeed to find herself so pleasantly situated. Her home was lovely, and her finances could hardly be considered straitened. Her husband was a generous, caring fellow, who truly seemed to have her best interests at heart. In time, they might even grow to love one another. She shuddered as she thought of what could have been. She could be tied to some despicable man, like Mr. Wickham.

No, she thought, *there are far worse places I could be than Cheventhorpe.*

Her husband happened to glance over in the midst of these ruminations and wondered what she could be thinking of to put such a serious expression upon her normally cheerful visage.

They arrived at their respective doors and Nathaniel reached out a hand to still Kitty as she made to open her door. She turned to him curiously.

"I failed to mention earlier that Hera comes with a stipulation. She is broken to side-saddle, but I would much prefer it if you would ride astride, for your own safety. With that in mind, you may find it necessary to have a few pairs of properly-fitting short pants made up for the purpose. Feel free to charge any expenses to my account. I hope you shall not mind my interference."

She contemplated his words, her head cocked to one side as a myriad emotions passed through her eyes. She was mildly irritated by his heavy-handedness in telling her what she could and could not do. But she could not bring herself to be truly angry with him. His concern for her well-being was endearing and his request was reasonable. She had an inkling that she might even grow to prefer riding astride once she had acquired some more suitable attire.

She smiled as she came to this conclusion and reached up to stroke his cheek gently. "I could not deny you something so easily done as that."

His breath hitched at her gesture and he found himself unable to move as she opened her door and disappeared inside, unfazed.

The same feat was not as easily accomplished by Nathaniel. His feet were rooted to the floor, leaden in his boots. Such a simple touch to have so great an effect. It shook him to his core. Dare he hope? He shook his head to clear it and made himself take a step forward and turn the doorknob.

His wife had no idea what she was doing to him.

*****

Nathaniel reemerged far sooner than his wife, changed and his mind already preoccupied with the ledgers that awaited him in his study. He had put them off for far too long already in order to enjoy the morning with his wife. He seated himself at his desk and pulled the first massive volume towards himself, immersing himself in the pages with a sigh.

When Lady Rockingham did emerge, it was to seek out her housekeeper with a request. It was one that could easily be granted, she found, and she left that lady's company well-pleased.

She retired to the library after that, taking comfort in a well-chosen book, as Elizabeth was oft to do. The absence of her sisters, although dulled by her husband's gracious presence that morning, was still felt keenly. As one is oft to do in such a case, she sought out the favorite activity of the person missed in an effort to ease her longing. Somehow knowing that Elizabeth was likely to be doing the exact same thing at that moment in Pemberley was of consolation to her.

Nathaniel found her there sometime later, having come to check on her when she had failed to heed the dinner bell. She was curled up on the sofa asleep, the book forgotten beside her. He almost could not bear to wake her, she looked so peaceful in slumber. He reached out to stroke back her hair, knowing as he did now that his touch would not wake her. She had had a late night to begin with, and the emotional toll of their dinner party and the subsequent tears had surely worn away at her usual stamina. He should not have been surprised to find her so.

He went to the door and summoned a lingering servant to request that their dinner be sent up to the mistress' sitting room. As the man strode down the hall to fulfill his task, Nathaniel turned back into the room and crossed to crouch before his wife. He laid one hand on her shoulder and shook her gently, calling her name softly in the still room.

But he had to increase his efforts to a much firmer shake before she even showed the beginnings of rousing. When she finally did open her eyes, it was to gaze about in confusion, the veil of sleep still heavy upon her.

Nathaniel smiled at her sleepy gaze. "There you are now, sleepyhead! I was beginning to fear you would never wake!"

She struggled to sit up and rubbed her eyes languorously with her fists. "What time is it?"

"The dinner bell rang some time ago. But I have instructed the staff that we shall dine in your sitting room. There is no need to stand on ceremony with just the pair of us, especially since you are fatigued. I expect you shall prefer to make it an early evening tonight."

She admitted this to be so and thanked him for his foresight and concern in looking out for her well-being. He held out a hand to help her to her feet, which she accepted gracefully.

He was loath to relinquish it, so instead he simply pulled her hand through his arm, keeping her delicate fingers securely covered with his own. Kitty snuck a glance at him from under her eyelashes, wondering at the gesture but too unsure of herself to question him.

They climbed the stairs together, and Kitty shyly led her husband through her bedchamber into the small adjoining sitting room. With a short while to pass until dinner would arrive, they settled into a pair of armchairs, Nathaniel reluctantly releasing his hold on her.

"Shall we have a game of checkers?" Nathaniel suggested as silence threatened to overtake them. This was thought to be a fine idea, so the board was brought and set before them. Thus, a pleasant half hour passed until their meal was served.

They settled themselves around the table, enjoying the soft ambience of the more intimate setting. The sun had begun its decline and treated them to a magnificent show as it sank, casting pools of yellow, orange, pink, and red about the room.

The changing light set Kate's chestnut curls on fire. Nathaniel struggled to drag his eyes away from her gleaming locks only to have them catch on her sparkling eyes. They held him captive, mesmerized. And yet she was unaware of the spell she held over him. She continued eating daintily, the daylight glinting off her silverware and scattering shards of light around the room.

He was loath to part with her at the evening's end. Even as dusk settled around them he struggled to pull himself from her company. Her light laughter as they continued their game after dinner was intoxicating and he found himself looking for ways to prolong it.

But even such a pleasant distraction had to come to an end eventually, and soon he found himself back on his side of the connecting door, longing to be with her still. It was with much reluctance he undressed and clambered into his own bed.

The massive piece engrossed him in its luxury, and yet it felt empty without Kate beside him. Now that he had held her in his arms and felt her breath upon his skin, his pillow was a poor substitute for a companion. He lay for hours it seemed, unable to find sleep, his eyes on the door that separated them and his heart calling out for her.

CHAPTER TEN

Kate hummed to herself as she set about pinning up her hair simply after her morning ride. Fanny had come to help her change out of her riding gear and gone already. She had declined the maid's assistance with her windswept hair, aware that her next destination did not require an intricate up-do. To the contrary, she felt it might actually do more harm than good to appear too much the wealthy mistress. To that end, she had chosen a simple, yet elegant, dress from her days as Kitty Bennet and styled her hair in an uncomplicated bun.

She hunted through her wardrobe for an apron, finally finding one hidden away in the back corner. She shook her head sadly. That just went to show how little work she had really done in the last month or so. She tucked the piece of fabric under her arm and shut the doors of the wardrobe.

She caught a glimpse of herself in the mirror as she turned to exit the room and smiled at her reflection. She looked the picture of a lady, but not so much so that she would intimidate. It was perfect.

Still humming, she exited her chambers and made her way to the stables, where a little phaeton and ponies waited for her, a basket of provisions already nestled on the floorboard. It was a pleasant day, with bright sunlight and a cool breeze. She guided the ponies on to the lane and let them continue to plod along, her hands lax on the lines as she lifted her face to catch the warmth of the sun's rays. She was pleased with the day, pleased with herself, and pleased with life in general.

She had forgotten how fulfilling it was to give of herself and help others. Lizzy and Jane had certainly tried to instill a sense of responsibility in her towards helping those less fortunate, especially during the months they had spent together at Pemberley and Chetborn. Kitty had often accompanied her sisters there on their errands of mercy. But she had gotten caught up in her own doubts and worries in the last few months and neglected any concerns but her own. It was past time for her to remedy that oversight.

She picked up the reins again and urged the reluctant ponies into a trot, whistling a jaunty tune as she made the turn out of the drive.

When she pulled up in the Robinson's yard, the same young boy who had held their horses the day before appeared around the corner. He went up to the dainty ponies and held their heads, murmuring softly to them as she clambered out of the phaeton. She noted how the animals' ears perked up at his voice and how they stilled under his calm hand.

"You have quite a way with horses, young man," she complimented him.

He flushed at the praise. "Thank ye, my Lady."

"Is your mother at home?" she asked.

"Yes, my Lady. She is just inside."

Kitty left her team in his capable hands, retrieved the basket from the floorboards, and crossed the yard to knock on the door of the humble cottage. It opened before she reached it and Mrs. Robinson appeared, outlined in the dim light of the doorway.

"Lady Rockingham, what a pleasant surprise." From the haggard look on Mrs. Robinson's face, it was anything but. She balanced a squalling toddler on one hip, the other hand supporting her aching back. Kitty could hear childish voices squabbling within.

Kitty hefted the heavy basket a little higher. "I hope you will forgive the imposition, Mrs. Robinson, of my calling so informally, but I have come to bring you some of the overflow from our kitchens. I thought it might be useful, with so many little mouths to feed."

The hard lines around the other woman's mouth softened and just the hint of a smile formed. "That would be much appreciated, my Lady. Please do come inside."

Kitty followed her inside and through to the tiny kitchen. She set down the laden basket on the kitchen table and motioned for the other woman to sit down.

"If you would be so kind as to direct me as to where everything goes, I would be more than happy to put it all away. It appears to me as if you could use a few minutes off your feet."

Mrs. Robinson admitted this to be so and gladly sat down on one of the chairs around the table, settling the toddler on what little of her lap was not taken up by her swollen midsection.

The three middle children had ceased their squabbling at the appearance of a lady in their home and followed their mother into the kitchen with wide eyes. They gathered around her skirts, too shy to do more than hide behind her, but too curious about this stranger to run off and play.

Kitty followed Mrs. Robinson's directions as to the proper place for each item in her basket, and soon the two women were chatting companionably.

The toddler, a little boy whom Kitty quickly deduced was named Henry, was not so subdued as his older siblings by her presence in the house. After a short while shifting restlessly on his mother's lap, he clambered to be let down. Once set on his feet, he waddled over to Kitty's side and held up his arms to be picked up.

Kitty could not resist his chubby little self. She grinned widely at his eager babbling and swept him up into her arms. "Well, are you not just the sweetest little chap."

He giggled and reached for the simple chain she wore around her neck. She thwarted his attempt by engulfing his little fist in her own and telling him with a smile, "No, m'dear. That does not belong to you."

Mrs. Robinson blushed and made to stand up. "I am so sorry, my Lady. I will take him from you."

Kitty quickly waved her back into her seat. "Nonsense. I love children." She settled the little chap on her hip and went back to putting away what little was left in the basket. When the last of the calf's foot jellies had been arranged neatly on the shelf Kitty turned to the lady of the house and asked, "Shall I make us some tea?"

The other woman smiled. "That sounds lovely." By this time the other children had started to lose interest and wandered away. James, the second eldest, disappeared outside to assist his older brother, Tom, with the chores and the two girls, in the middle at six and four years of age, drifted into the corner to play quietly with their dolls.

Kitty put the kettle on to heat and settled at the table to wait. Little Henry snuggled sleepily into the crook of her arm and popped his thumb into his mouth.

Mrs. Robinson, or Alice, as she insisted Kitty call her, leaned back in her seat and rested a hand lightly on her rounded belly. "I think this is the most peaceful we have been in a fortnight."

Kitty laughed. "Sometimes I wish for a little noise at Cheventhorpe. I was one of five sisters. Our house was never quiet. Now I do not know what to do with myself with that great empty house all to myself."

Alice's gaze drifted to the toddler on Kitty's lap and she grinned. "Mayhap you will soon have some little ones of your own and then your home will resonate with sound. You certainly have a way with them."

Kitty looked down at the little boy. "Maybe someday. I honestly had not given it much thought. There have been so many changes to adjust to just becoming Lady Rockingham that I have not put much thought into the future."

"I imagine there have been a great many changes in your life in the last few months," Alice acknowledged.

Kitty's smile was strained. "You have no idea. One would not think it to be so difficult a transition to make."

"It is always difficult to leave behind those we love for the unknown. But in the end, sometimes the things that are most difficult in life are the most worthwhile." She caressed her stomach and smiled to herself. "If I had never left behind my family and married Edmond, I would never have known my beautiful children."

Kitty rose at the sound of the water boiling and put the tea in to steep. She hovered nearby while she waited. "I am sure you are right."

She poured them both a cup of tea and settled back at the table to continue their chat. Henry was soon asleep on her lap and she found herself lingering, reluctant to give up the comfort of his warm little body cuddled against her. But she could not in good conscience keep Alice from the myriads of tasks she knew must need her attention for her own convenience, so she grudgingly roused Henry enough to hand him off to his mother to be laid down for a nap. She excused herself with a promise to return in a few days' time to assist with the large pile of mending she was sure Alice never saw the bottom of.

The older woman followed her out to stand in the doorway and wave good-bye, her children appearing again to gather round her skirts and wave shyly.

As she left the family behind her, she could not help but reflect on the picture they painted of domestic felicity. Sure, at times it was bound to be rowdy and loud, people shouting over each other and vying for attention, but Kitty had been raised in that environment. She enjoyed a lively atmosphere.

She smiled as she envisioned Cheventhorpe with a family in it. The house would not seem so cavernous and empty with children's laughter to brighten its gloomy interior. In her mind's eye, she pictured a little boy and a little girl. The little boy had the same rugged good looks just beginning to show in his childish features as Nathaniel and the little girl had her wild hair and green eyes. Her heart warmed as she imagined their home filled with light and love.

There was only one problem with that picture.

The smile faded from her face as the truth of the matter smacked her in the face and settled in a leaden lump on her chest. She swallowed hard against the sudden constriction in her throat.

Nathaniel did not love her. And he probably never would.

CHAPTER ELEVEN

Nathaniel was waiting impatiently for the return of his wife, pacing anxiously by the windows overlooking the lane. She had left without giving him any hint of where she was going or what her plans were. She had not even informed him she was leaving. He was fortunate he had looked up from his ledgers in time to see her driving off, or he would have supposed her to be still in the house somewhere.

He was too proud to resort to asking the servants what his wife's activities were. Instead, he paced. He was becoming dangerously close to wearing a path in the carpets by the time she returned.

He breathed a sigh of relief to see her drive up the lane, safe and sound. He clattered down the staircase to meet her, pausing on the last step as she came in. He tried desperately to appear nonchalant. "Oh, Kate, there you are. I wondered where you had got off to."

She looked up at him with a watery smile that told him instantly something was the matter. "I went to bring some things to Mrs. Robinson. I did not suppose you would mind." The light was gone from her eyes. She barely made eye contact before looking away dejectedly.

"No. No, I have no objections," Nathaniel murmured, confused by her manner and searching her face for some explanation.

Her refusal to meet his eyes prevented him from any further discoveries. He descended the last step to take her hand gently in his own.

She snatched it back. "If you will excuse me, I find myself fatigued from this morning's activities. I think I will rest for awhile." She pushed passed him to ascend the stairs without a backward glance.

Nathaniel stared after her retreating back and rounded shoulders until she passed out of his sight down the hall. What in the world had he done now?

*****

Kate berated herself as she traversed the empty hallways to her chambers. His tender touch had almost been her undoing. But it was no more than the concern of a friend. That was all she was to him. Had he not told her so, back in London?

Regardless of how much she might long to experience his love, to share more than a house and a title, it was not to be. She would do well to accept her fate and learn to be content with it.

But that thought did not stop the tears that threatened from slipping unbidden down her cheeks.

*****

Nathaniel stood frozen on the staircase for several minutes after Kate had left, his mind whirring with possibilities before settling on one determination. The cough of a footman in the entry below brought him back to reality. He turned to follow his wife.

His footsteps on the treads were heavy. What was he to say? He did not know. All he knew was that he could not run from his responsibility toward her. If he was the cause of her turmoil, then he must take action to fix it. He could not shirk his duty just to save face.

And if he was not to blame, then he would be there to comfort her. A man did no less for his wife. He had to try.

He made the turn into the corridor their quarters were off of and paused outside her door. He stood there quietly, hoping for he knew what not. The heavy wood door revealed none of Kate's secrets. He sighed and went through his own door.

Within moments he stood on his side of their connecting door, his ear pressed against the wood. She was doing a good job of muffling her tears, but Nathaniel knew what to listen for now.

His heart wrenched at the sound. He knocked lightly. "Kate?"

The quiet noises abruptly stopped and he could tell she was struggling to gain some semblance of composure before she answered him. Her voice still trembled when she responded, "Yes?"

"Have I done something to upset you?" he asked hesitantly, not sure he really wanted to know the answer.

She barked a self-deprecating laugh through her tears. "No, Nathaniel. I am fine. I have just come to a rather unpleasant realization. Please, go back to your ledgers." Her voice was firm. She did not want him. She was shutting him out.

Nathaniel slid down the length of the door to sit with his back against the solid wood. He tipped his head back to rest on the door. The sound of her crying filtered to him. The door stood stalwart between them, a barrier he could not seem to surmount despite his best efforts.

How had she managed to destroy all the progress they had made in a few moments? He longed to cry tears of frustration along with his wife. Instead, he turned his thoughts to a possible solution. He would not despair.

He loved his wife. He just had to earn her love and trust in return.

*****

Kitty descended the stairs for dinner, fully prepared to pretend like nothing had ever happened. The only evidence of the afternoon she had spent crying was a slight puffiness and redness around her eyes.

Nathaniel was only too happy to go along with her charade, unsure of how to broach such a difficult topic anyway. They sat down at the table, silence stretching between them.

Nathaniel waited until the first course had been served and the servants had retreated from the room before he made any effort to break the silence. "I have taken the liberty of arranging a picnic for us tomorrow."

Kitty's head snapped up in surprise. "You have? Whatever for?" She blushed as she realized how her words sounded. "Er, what I mean is, do you not have some estate business to care for on the morrow?"

"I will always have some estate business that could monopolize my attention," Nathaniel acknowledged. "But I thought it would be a nice opportunity for us to spend some more time together."

Kitty swallowed hard. Her husband was certainly not making things easy for her. She remembered their ride only a few days ago, when their attraction had threatened to get the better of them. Her cheeks flushed scarlet and she had trouble meeting Nathaniel's eyes.

Still, she could not very well turn him down, and she doubted very much he would allow her to anyway. His jaw was set determinedly as he waited for her response.

"I see," she murmured. "Very well then, I suppose that could be a pleasant respite."

He grinned broadly at her acquiescence, and she blinked at the intensity of the joy in his expression. "Good."

They returned to their food, Nathaniel digging in whole-heartedly now that his objective was reached. Kate wondered at his joy in her response. When had her acceptance come to mean so much to her husband?

*****

Nathaniel whistled an easy tune to himself as he tested the straps holding their picnic luncheon securely to his saddle. He was pleased with himself for getting Kate to agree to an outing so easily. He had honestly expected her to put up more of a fight to the idea, given her reaction to him earlier.

He hummed a bar and grinned. He was looking forward to today, with every expectation of progress in his wooing efforts being made. He would not allow them to backtrack, not when they had come so far, and not when he had finally realized what he wanted in their relationship.

Abaccus pricked his ears up and swung his head around to look towards the house, his interest caught by the appearance of Kate in her new riding outfit.

Nathaniel could see the maids had been busy. He was kind of sad to see his old, outgrown short pants go; she had been so ridiculously adorable in them. He had to admit though, that this new, tailored pair accentuated some of his wife's assets in ways that the old ones had hidden.

He watched her approach appreciatively, unable to tear his eyes away. The sudden hush of the normally bustling stable yard told him he was not the only one to notice. He turned to scowl upon the yard full of men ogling his wife.

Most of them turned away hurriedly and busied themselves with chores, but the head groom standing nearby dropped him a quick wink. "Caught yourself a right good 'un, did ye."

Nathaniel could not help but laugh and acknowledge the man's good-natured teasing. Kate came upon them then, and the other man doffed his hat to grace her with a slight bow before excusing himself, a twinkle still in his eye.

Nathaniel turned to his wife, who had raised one eyebrow quizzically. "What was that all about?"

He grinned. "Nothing important."

She looked like she did not believe him for a moment, but she let his answer pass unchallenged. Instead she turned her attention to Abaccus, who was vying for her attention by pushing his head against her arm insistently. She reached up to rub under his forelock and murmured, "Yes, old boy, I see you."

Abaccus preened under her attention, arching his neck and whinnying loudly. She laughed at his display and turned to Nathaniel. "Are you ready to set off?"

"As soon as you are."

"Let us mount up then." She moved towards her own horse, paying Hera the same attentions she had bestowed upon Abaccus before leading her over to one of the mounting blocks to mount up.

Once they were both settled in their saddles, Nathaniel led the way out of the stable yard and on to a little-traveled path that would lead them to the secluded area he had in mind for their picnic. The path, although not well-traveled, was wide enough for them to ride two abreast, so once they were sufficiently well enough underway, Nathaniel reined in Abaccus to allow Kate and Hera to catch up with them.

"I noticed you received a letter in the post this morning," Nathaniel commented. "Was it from one of your sisters?"

Kitty beamed at the remembrance. "It was from Lizzy. I daresay I will receive one from Jane soon enough as well, as she has always been a far more reliable correspondent."

"What does she write?" Nathaniel asked.

"Oh, the usual things. Lizzy is very witty, you know, and quite the studier of characters. She paints a rather humorous portrait of their new rector. The poor man appears to be an earnest, sincere fellow, but she writes that he has a rather tedious tendency to go on long moral rampages. I wish you had had the opportunity to get to know my sisters better while we were all in London."

"I found them both to be very pleasant whilst we were all in company together."

"Yes, they are very diverting." She quieted, a sweet, nostalgic smile still upon her lips, even as her mind was far away.

Nathaniel watched her face, yearning to be thought of by her with as much fondness. "You should invite them for a visit at their earliest convenience."

She turned her gaze back upon him, one corner of her mouth quirking up sadly. "I am afraid their earliest convenience is still many months away. They are both expecting in the fall. It is far more likely that *we* shall be waiting upon *them* before they will be available to travel here."

"You should like to visit them upon their lying-in, I expect?" he asked.

"Yes, very much so. They are so closely situated that we shall be able to see them both, I should think. In fact, I should not be surprised if instead of remaining apart as their time draws near, they choose to spend it together at either

Chetborn or Pemberley. Then I shall be able to attend them both at once!"

Kate sounded so cheered by the prospect that Nathaniel could not help but smile. "We shall plan on it then."

She rewarded him with a full blown smile that nearly caused him to drop his reins. She reached a hand out to bridge the distance between them. He let her take his rough hand in her dainty clasp. She squeezed it with surprising strength and said a heartfelt, "Thank you."

Nathaniel was ridiculously pleased with himself for garnering her favor. He squeezed her hand in return and was slightly disappointed when she pulled it away and turned back to guiding Hera. He should have taken the opportunity to lace his fingers through hers and hold her hand captive within his own. But it was too late now; the opportunity was lost. He searched his mind for ways to incite her to repeat the gesture, but came up empty-handed. It would have to suffice for the moment.

She went on, oblivious to his ruminations. "I find myself looking forward to having little nieces or nephews, although I am sure they will be quite spoilt. Are you?"

Nathaniel had never thought of her sisters' pregnancies resulting in nieces and nephews for *him* before. The unexpected idea made him smile. Although there might not be any children for him in the near future, at least he would have the privilege of becoming an uncle twice over! He felt suddenly what it meant to be a part of Kitty's family. He had no other siblings; there would be no nieces and nephews on his side. By marrying her, he had automatically inherited them.

His heart warmed and his chest swelled with pride at the thought of those little upturned faces calling him, "Uncle."

He smiled. "Yes, I suppose I am."

Kitty heard the pride in his voice and looked over at him with a chuckle and a raised eyebrow. "Do not let it go to your head now."

Nathaniel mirrored her expression, his eyes teasing. "An uncle is just as allowed to be proud of his nieces and nephews as their aunt is."

She laughed outright. "Very well then. I give you leave to be very proud indeed." She sighed wistfully. "I cannot wait to behold their chubby cheeks and cuddle them close. Any child of Jane's is sure to be beautiful, and Lizzy's is bound to be obnoxiously intelligent."

The talk of babies inevitably brought Nathaniel's mind around to picturing their own children. He quickly quelled the mental images that sprang to mind, knowing now was neither the time nor place to indulge in such fantasies.

He chimed in, "Let us hope that the Bingleys' infant does not inherit Charles' ginger hair."

Kitty giggled. "No, but I should think that to be adorable! Can you not picture it? And sticking straight up, too!"

He had to admit she was right. He grinned widely. "But he shall be teased horribly when he goes away to school."

"Never!" Kitty asserted. "He will be far too good-natured and well-liked."

"That is quite likely, given his parents," Nathaniel agreed. "I am amazed the servants do not cheat them out of half of their income."

Kate snickered. "That is what Pappa said would happen when Bingley applied to him for her hand."

Nathaniel snuck a glance at her sideways. "I am afraid to think what he must have said about us then."

Kitty frowned at the mention of his application for her hand and feigned a sudden interest in the surrounding foliage. Her change of demeanor caught Nathaniel's attention. What he had meant to be teasing had become anything but. He reached over to cross the distance between them and pulled back gently on her reins, bringing their mounts to a standstill. Kitty turned her head to send him a quizzical glance.

"What is wrong?" he asked gently.

She frowned and averted her eyes again. "Nothing in particular." She tried to urge Hera into motion again, but Nathaniel's steady hands on the reins held her still. Kitty harrumphed at his manner but did not bother making any more futile attempts.

He tried again to get her to open up. "What is wrong? What did your Father say?"

She stubbornly refused to meet his eyes and bit out sharply, "He said I shall have more fine clothes and carriages than Jane and Lizzy together." There was more to the story than that, Nathaniel could tell, but he also realized he was not to hear it right then. He reluctantly released his hold on the reins and silently reminded himself to be patient with her.

They resumed their forward progress. Nathaniel let the silence stretch between them until he could see her stance was softening as they rode. "You can certainly afford them," Nathaniel commented slowly, unsure of how she would react to his words. "But I very much doubt that is all he had to say about our situation."

A wry smile tugged at the corners of her mouth and when she looked at him he could read the embarrassment and apology in her eyes. "He also said my mother would be overjoyed at my acquisition of a title."

Nathaniel remembered that woman's reaction and felt his own mouth turn up. He shook his head. "I think it is safe to say that statement was accurate."

Kitty sighed. She did not want to remember her father's reaction to her engagement. He had never been one to show much interest in any of his daughters, with the exception of

Lizzy. But somehow, she had expected more of him in the moment. Surely, he must care for her, even just a little, as his own flesh and blood. But he had seemed so utterly unfeeling and uncaring of her fate that day.

She supposed, as it related to his own comfort, her fate was unimportant. What father could ask more for his daughter than that she be comfortably situated with a home of her own? She had never been much more than a silly little girl to him in comparison with the bright Lizzy. Now, she was just one less mouth to feed, one less daughter to worry about providing a dowry for, one less woman to intrude on his privacy and solace.

In his eyes, he had done very well by her. He had secured for her a comfortable home and a good income with a reputable gentleman. Perhaps she had been naïve to want more.

Nathaniel could not know where her thoughts had taken her. All he knew was she had been silent for far too long, and he yearned to hear her bright laughter and see her carefree smile again. He could not allow her to slip into melancholy.

He reached over to tug on the simple braid she had slung over one shoulder in lieu of a more elaborate hairstyle. The teasing gesture drew her attention. She raised one eyebrow at him as he smiled a crooked grin.

"There is a nice straight stretch just up ahead," he offered. "What say you to a race?"

He was rewarded with an immediate, brilliant smile. A race was the perfect remedy for her disconsolate thoughts. She could barely restrain herself until the aforementioned straight appeared before them.

She was off like a shot before Nathaniel could even start a countdown. He laughed at her eagerness and unnecessarily urged his mount faster. Abaccus was not one to be outdone, especially not by the new mare in the stable. He could feel the stallion's stride lengthening beneath him and their picnic lunch thudding rhythmically against his leg as the animal surged forward to close the distance.

Kate glanced back over her shoulder at them and urged Hera faster as they approached, but it was too late. Abaccus drew nearer, right on their heels, then to Hera's flank, until finally they were neck and neck as the end of the stretch was fast approaching.

Each animal was not to be defeated by the other. They fought for the lead, but neither was able to pull ahead before they were forced to slow. They were perfectly matched. Just as he and Kate were.

*****

The pure rush of adrenaline from the race had worked its magic on Kate. She was giggling and giddy as they pulled up their mounts. Nathaniel could not help but laugh with her. Her joy was contagious.

He touched her hand and directed her attention ahead where the tree line broke to reveal an open field. "Come on. Our destination is not far."

They left the wooded lane behind them and crossed the field to where a babbling brook wound its way through, one giant old oak standing guard over its banks. They removed their horses' tack and turned them out to graze under their watchful eye. Nathaniel spread a large blanket under the oak's sheltering branches and helped Kitty settle down on it.

She did not stay seated long. The brook drew her like a fly to honey. She cast an impish grin over her shoulder at Nathaniel, who remained seated on the blanket, and slipped out of her riding boots and stockings. She left them in a pile among the tree roots and rolled up her short pants before wading into the clear water. The water was not much over knee high in its deepest areas, and where she stood in the shallows it only reached to just above her ankles.

She watched, fascinated, as a few curious minnows swam up to inspect her toes. She giggled as their slippery bodies tickled her skin. The crisp waters still held some of the chill of winter and her toes quickly turned numb, forcing her to climb out reluctantly and rejoin Nathaniel.

He reclined on the blanket, his torso supported against the tree as he watched her play in the water with amusement and then, as she came to join him, with appreciation. She settled beside him, close enough to touch, yet far enough away they would not accidentally brush against each other as they moved.

Her bare feet and ankles captivated him. He would never have thought he would find a woman's extremities to be so appealing.

Kate noticed the focus of his intent gaze and blushed under his scrutiny. She tucked her feet demurely under herself to hide them from his gaze. Nathaniel was not so easily dissuaded. The sole of one foot still peeped out at him, tantalizing him with its nearness. With a devilish grin, he reached out a finger to stroke the length of her foot, watching in delight as her toes curled under his ticklish touch.

She giggled and pulled her foot away from him. "Stop that!"

He just grinned and reached for her foot again. She snatched it out of his reach and scrambled backward with a gasp as he advanced on her, a teasing glint in his eye.

She laughed as his fingers found her ribcage, revealing another ticklish spot. He gleefully exploited her weakness, leaving her breathless and winded beneath his hands. He collapsed onto his side beside her, propping up his head with one hand as he surveyed her flushed face with satisfaction.

Kitty flipped on her stomach once she had caught her breath. She shot an exasperated glance in Nathaniel's direction. "Was that really necessary?"

He grinned. "No, but it was fun."

She stuck her tongue out at him playfully. He laughed and bridged the distance between them to tenderly tuck a strand of hair that had come loose from her braid behind her ear. She sucked in a breath at his touch and caught her lower lip between her teeth. She looked up at him shyly through the thick fringe of her lashes. His fingers lingered on her skin as their eyes caught and held.

Kate cleared her throat and lowered her eyes as the intensity of his gaze threatened to envelop her. She did not dare guess what he was thinking. She rose and started toward the basket containing their luncheon. "Are you hungry?"

Nathaniel let her make her escape, for the moment. "Famished."

Kate rifled through the basket and examined its contents before laying out the provisions. She could tell care had been taken to select her favorite foods. Whether that was on the part of the cook, who appreciated her taste in food, or on Nathaniel's part, she could not say.

They fell to eating, interspersed with some pleasant, inane conversation. Kate tried to steer the discussion away from anything too personal, afraid of where that path might lead them. They were teetering on the edge of something, and she was not sure if she was ready to take the plunge and see where this, whatever *this* was, would take them.

There was too much at stake to take the next step lightly. She was putting her heart at risk. It was a scary thing to open herself up to such hurt. She knew if she let herself love him, as it would be so easy to do, and he did not return her feelings, it would crush her.

She was afraid to let herself hope for a future with him.

Their stomachs full, they laid back on the blanket and basked in the sunlight that filtered through the branches. The warm, hazy day belied the chill of the water. The burbling brook and gentle breeze soon lulled them into slumber.

Nathaniel was the first to wake, quite awhile later. He stretched and cast his eyes about, perplexed as to what had woke him. The sky had turned to overcast and there was a sudden chill in the air. But that in itself was not enough to wake him. Kitty was still fast asleep a few feet from him, curled up on her side. Her peaceful repose made him yearn to cuddle up beside her and wrap his arms around her, but he held back. Instead, his gaze was drawn to their mounts.

Abaccus stood head up, ears pricked, his focus firmly fixed to the west. Nathaniel turned his attention to Hera. She was pawing the ground uneasily and pulling against her restraints. Something was wrong. Nathaniel frowned and followed Abaccus' gaze towards the west. His heart skipped a beat as he noticed black clouds gathering above the tree line. As he watched, a flash of lightning split the air, followed closely by a deafening crack of thunder he could feel reverberating through his chest.

Instantly, he knew with a certainty what had woke him. He turned urgently to roughly shake Kate awake. There was no time to waste waking her gently. She would probably sleep through the storm if he let her. It felt like an eternity before she finally peeled her eyelids apart. He recognized the flash of annoyance that sparked through her eyes at being woken so rudely, and spoke quickly to dispel any animosity, "There is a storm approaching, Kate. We need to get back to the house, and quickly." Another rumble of thunder lent credibility to his words.

She sat up, tousled and still only half awake. He was tempted to lean in and take advantage of her state to steal a kiss, but the nearing storm stopped him in his tracks. He hurriedly began saddling up their mounts, while Kitty roused sufficiently enough to fold up the blanket and start packing up their picnic basket.

He finished securing the basket and turned to find Kitty searching frantically through the grass. "What are you looking for?" he asked irritably, impatient to be on their way.

"I cannot find my stockings and riding boots," she snapped, just as irritably. Was it not obvious?

He glanced down at her feet and realized she was still barefoot. He groaned and joined in the hunt. Surely they could not be far.

He finally found them among the tree roots, but by now the storm was almost upon them. He tried to calm the horses while Kate pulled them on. Hera was neighing loudly and pulling against the reins where he had looped them around the tree branches. Her eyes were white with fear and she trembled under his hand. Abaccus was also obviously displeased with his current predicament, but he at least did not seem so completely terrified.

Making a snap decision, he threw Kate up on his own mount. She opened her mouth to protest, but one shake of his head silenced her as he clambered onto Hera's back. Thank goodness he had insisted his wife ride astride! The mare fought him for control, wild with fear, but his firm hand managed to keep her from rearing up and dislodging him from the saddle. His heart pounding and barely in control of his mount, he urged the mare forward and set off down the lane, Kate in hot pursuit.

They were not close to the house. Even moving at as fast a pace as he dared through the trees, the rain was already beginning to fall as they reached the opening to the stable yard. It came down in sheets, drenching them to the skin as they urged their mounts to the safety of the stables. Stable boys and grooms ran out to grab their bridles and Nathaniel quickly dismounted, flinging the reins to a waiting groom while running around Hera to assist Kitty off Abaccus. He pulled her into the relative safety of the stables to wait for the storm to pass, while the servants cared for their mounts.

The stable was cozy and dry in comparison to the storm that raged around them. He took several deep breaths and willed his heart to stop racing. Beside him, Kate shivered uncontrollably, soaked to the skin. Her wet clothes clung to her like a second skin, outlining every curve and rise of her body. He pulled her into his embrace and rubbed his hands briskly up and down her arms, willing some of his body heat to warm her sufficiently until they could cross to the house and change into dry clothes. He spared no thought for the intimacy of such an act, only the comfort it might provide her.

As violent as the storm had been, it passed just as quickly. Nathaniel breathed a sigh of relief as the last of the raindrops subsided and the air cleared. Kitty still shivered under his touch. "Come. I think it is safe to return to the house now."

He did not relinquish her hand as they crossed to the house. They were met at the door with blankets by Mrs. Davis. She fretted over their appearance and sent them up the stairs to change, calling up as an afterthought, "My Lord, the Dowager Lady Rockingham is in the blue parlor. She was passing by when the storm came up and sought refuge here."

Nathaniel paused on the stairs while Kate kept going. "Please inform her I shall be down to receive her shortly."

They hurried up to their rooms now that they had a guest to entertain, Kate heartedly grateful that she had not been caught so outrageously dressed by her elegant mother-in-law, even if it was Nathaniel's fault.

Fanny was already waiting for her in her room when she arrived. The heat from the freshly stoked fire was a welcome relief, as she still had yet to warm up, despite Nathaniel's ministrations. She was quickly stripped out of her wet clothes and set by the fire, wrapped in her dressing gown and a warm blanket, while Fanny set about briskly drying her hair with a towel.

The warmth flooding through her body coupled with the exhaustion surfacing after their adrenaline rush of a ride would have quickly lulled her to sleep if not for their guest downstairs. As soon as she was dry enough, Fanny helped her into a fresh gown and sat her down at the dressing table to wrangle her wind-tousled curls into submission.

Nathaniel knocked on the connecting door while they were in the midst of that fiasco. Kitty called out, "Come in!"

He peeked around the door, noticed she was dressed, and came in to sit at the foot of the bed and wait for them to finish.

Kate's brow furrowed with worry at his appearance. "If you would prefer not to leave your mother waiting as long, you can go down without me."

Nathaniel shook his head. "No. She would not expect me to, and it appears that you are finishing up."

Fanny took one of the pins out of her mouth and tried to fasten a curl in place. Kate sighed. "We are trying, but the wet weather has made my hair particularly unruly, I fear."

Nathaniel noted with appreciation the cascade of curls down her back. "It looks beautiful to me the way it is. I do not understand why you should try to fight it so."

Kate fidgeted in her seat. "I do not want to appear unladylike in front of your mother. She is so dignified and poised."

Nathaniel laughed. "If you had seen the way she would play with me as a child you would not think that. Besides, she loves you already. There is no reason to fear her."

Kate sighed and Fanny placed the last pin triumphantly. "There my Lady! You are ready to go down."

She stood and turned to face her husband. He rose and held out his arm for her to take. Together, they descended to the blue parlor. Kate was glad for Nathaniel's presence by her side. As agreeable as she found her mother-in-law to be, she still felt some trepidation facing the great lady. She had after all, taken her place as the new Lady Rockingham. She could only hope she was living up to the title.

Her thoughts engaged elsewhere, she would have made a wrong turn in Cheventhorpe's maze of hallways if not for Nathaniel's gentle pressure on her arm leading her in the right direction.

When they finally stood outside of the blue parlor, Kitty was half surprised that Nathaniel's mother was still inside. She rose gracefully from her seat on the settee to greet them. Nathaniel went forward to embrace her gently and give her a peck on the cheek. "It is a pleasure to see you, Mother. I apologize for neglecting you. We were caught in the storm this afternoon and were in no state to receive company."

Cecelia waved away his apology. "It is completely understandable, my dear." She turned her attention to Kate, bestowing a truly delighted smile upon her. "I am happy that such an unfortunate occasion has given us a chance to spend some time together."

Kate smiled back, put at ease once again by Cecelia's friendly demeanor. "I hope you will stay to dinner."

"I would be delighted."

*****

Kate surveyed the spread laid before them at dinner and was pleased to note she had selected a good meal for that night, especially with the arrival of their unexpected guest. Mrs. Davis had never led her wrong yet with her suggestions, although she could not reasonably give her credit for the inclement weather. Kate was grateful for her experience in running the household, as it more than adequately made up for her own lack thereof.

Cecelia, too, was pleased with the quality of the food. She complimented Kate on her selections. "You have become quite proficient at entertaining, I see. I should not be surprised if you should decide to hold a ball soon."

Kate's eyes lit up at the prospect of a ball. She turned to her husband. "I had not thought of that! Do you suppose we could hold a ball?"

Nathaniel was taken aback by his wife's enthusiasm. After the trepidation that had consumed her over throwing a simple dinner party, he would have assumed hosting a ball would have been far too overwhelming an undertaking.

"Do you think you would be up to it?" he asked hesitantly.

She bounced slightly in her seat. "Of course! I love balls! Do say we can hold a ball!"

Nathaniel had never seen her like this. He answered slowly, half afraid to agree to it, "I do not see why we cannot, if you would really like to."

She squealed and barely restrained herself from rushing around the table to give him an excited hug.

Cecelia laughed at her fervor and Nathaniel's apprehension. "I assure you, Nathaniel, that is quite a typical reaction for any young lady when presented with the opportunity for a ball. I have been known to look forward to them myself."

Nathaniel shook his head. He learned new things about his wife every day. "Do you like to dance?" he asked, with a sinking feeling that he already knew what her answer would be.

Her eyes widened. "Of course!"

He forced a smile to his face. Cecelia smiled sympathetically and reached over to pat his hand reassuringly. "It may not be your favorite activity, dear, but I am sure your wife would be more than willing to practice with you."

Kate cocked her head and surveyed him seriously. "Do you not like to dance?"

He smiled ruefully. "As my mother said, it is not my favorite activity. I lack a sense of rhythm, which makes it a decidedly more difficult endeavor."

"But not an impossible one," Kate pointed out. "I should be very glad to practice with you. I expect you would be a most amiable partner."

"You will not think that when I am stepping on your toes."

Kate laughed. "I grant you, you may not be the most comfortable partner. But at least you will be a good-looking one." As soon as the words left her mouth, she seemed to realize what she had said. She blushed red to the roots of her hair and caught her bottom lip beneath her teeth, peeking up from under her lashes shyly at her husband.

Nathaniel grinned broadly at her fumble and Cecelia tried to hide her smile behind her napkin. "I am glad I can oblige," Nathaniel responded with a smirk.

Kate glared at him and his gloating and then determinedly changed the topic as she waited for her cheeks to cool. She turned to Cecelia. "Where were you headed earlier when the storm caught you by surprise?"

Cecelia shot a laughing glance in her son's direction, but answered composedly, giving her daughter-in-law a chance to recover.

The rest of the evening passed pleasantly, with light conversation and only a few lingering smirks from Nathaniel. When Cecelia departed for her own home late that night, it was with the understanding that she would return in a few day's time to help Kate begin planning for the ball.

The Marquess and Marchioness turned to head inside as the dowager Lady Rockingham's carriage disappeared down the drive. Nathaniel was still puffed with pleasure from Kate's earlier compliment. So, she found him handsome… that was certainly a step in the right direction. He could not stop the grin that spread slowly across his face.

"So when do you suggest to give your handsome husband his dancing lessons?" he teased.

Kate blushed again and shoved him playfully. "When you get that ego of yours under control!" She turned and ran lightly up the stairs, only pausing on the landing to call back a laughing good night.

Nathaniel rocked back on his heels and happily hummed a few bars under his breath. If he was a betting man, which he was not, he would say things were actually proceeding a little better than planned.

He grinned and followed his wife up the stairs.

CHAPTER TWELVE

The next day would prove to be a busy one in the Rockingham household. Kitty was up early in anticipation of all that had to be done. She was pleased to have her day filled with activity. It was nice to feel productive for once. With a household full of servants, it was easy to be caught sitting around, twiddling her thumbs. But her sisters were not ones to remain idle when there was work to be accomplished, and she was determined not to be either. Delegating was one thing, laziness was another entirely.

Her first order of business was to meet with Mrs. Davis about the household affairs and to discreetly inquire as to her suggestions for a ball. The other woman seemed enticed by the prospect and readily took up the challenge. Kate could see the wheels starting to turn and her eyes lighting up with glee as the housekeeper thought over the idea.

While Kate would wait until Cecelia returned to start the official preparations, she thought it prudent to begin soliciting the advice and help of the household servants. Mrs. Davis, she was sure, would prove to be invaluable in the process.

She departed for the breakfast table satisfied with their interview and assured of the success of her ball. She was the first to arrive in the room, as her husband had been cornered by his steward for a lengthy discussion on crop rotation. She passed the open door of his study with some amusement, as the man's monotonous voice droning on reached her ears. A quick glance inside revealed her husband, twirling a quill impatiently as he politely tried to appear interested in what his steward was saying.

She gave him a little wave when her movement as she passed the door caught his attention. He perked up in his seat and gave her a little half-smile before turning his full attention to the man before him. The corners of her mouth quirked up as she continued down the hallway. She fully expected him to abandon the poor man and follow her into the breakfast room, and she was not disappointed.

Having instructed his steward to do as he saw fit and then summarily dismissing him, Nathaniel appeared shortly thereafter. He was whistling as he crossed the threshold, and smiled a warm welcome at his wife as she served herself from the sideboard. He approached her. "If you would prefer to sit down, I will finish filling your plate for you."

She accepted his offer, instructing him as to her preferences among what was laid out and then retreating to her seat at the breakfast table to read the society column of the papers.

Nathaniel smiled as he came to join her, bearing their plates. She looked up somewhat guiltily at being caught reading something so trivial, but Nathaniel did not berate her choice of reading material. Instead, he offered her the plate of food and picked up another section of the paper for his own perusal.

Kate eagerly scanned the wedding announcements and allowed herself to be drawn into the world of balls and debutantes. She knew what it was to dream of dresses and dances and handsome gentlemen.

She glanced up at the man across the table from her and sighed. She did not regret how things had ended up for her. Her husband was a fine man, and the only thing lacking in their marriage was the love that could truly bind them together as man and wife. It was more than could be said for the majority of society's married couples. But sometimes she could not help but miss the expectation, the excitement of not knowing what the future held.

She envied those debutantes their rose-colored glasses and their hopes for the future. Her own future was set in stone. She was the Marchioness of Rockingham, regardless of whether her husband loved her or not. She might hope for a change in his feelings, but there was no guarantee it would ever take place. She could never again look at the world as she once had, full of promise and adventure. There were too many uncertainties in reality. She smiled wryly. Life was not a gothic romance novel.

She cast her gaze back over the print. She did not recognize any of the names before her. But she felt keenly their anticipation. Slowly, a satisfied smile crept across her face. She may know where her future lay, but she still had a ball and dresses and dances to look forward to. Her gaze moved to rest on Nathaniel, who was still absorbed in his paper. There was even a handsome gentleman to factor into the equation.

And unlike all those giggling debutantes, who could only dream of a dashing husband, she was bound by matrimony to a swoon-worthy gentleman of her very own. None could lay claim to him but her.

There was some pride in that, to know that he belonged solely to her. Regardless of how others might have fought for his affections or favor, he was tied irreversibly to her.

Nathaniel looked up at that moment, to catch her watching him with an indecipherable look in her eye. He cocked his head curiously and then glanced down his front. "Have I spilled coffee down my waist coat?"

Kate gave herself a little shake and a light blush stole across her cheeks. "No. No, you have not. I was just thinking."

"Well then, what were you thinking so seriously about?"

She sought desperately for something plausible to say without revealing her real thoughts and grinned when she found it. "I was wondering when we could fit in your dance lesson today."

Nathaniel scowled at the reminder but quickly overcame his distaste for the activity at the prospect of spending more time one-on-one with his wife. "Whenever you should like."

"I have promised to return to Mrs. Robinson's to help her with some mending this morning, after our ride. But I should be able to work with you when I return."

"That should be sufficient. I expect I will be shut up with the ledgers most of the day, so when you are ready you can come find me in the study and we can adjourn to the ballroom."

She agreed that his proposal was acceptable and they returned to their papers, sneaking glances at each other over the tops of the open pages when they thought the other was not looking.

Kate could not help the small smile that appeared at the thought of sharing a dance with her husband. Despite his claims to the contrary, she knew that someone who moved with such grace on horseback could not be completely flummoxed on the dance floor. There was a natural rhythm to a horse's gait that a rider must move in harmony with, just as there was in the steps of a dance. If she could help him make the connection between the two, she had no doubt that he would easily pick up the various dances.

She glanced up at him over the top of her paper and caught him staring at her, an appreciative gleam in his eye. She wondered where his thoughts lay, and blushed at the realization they were turned most decidedly towards her.

Nathaniel found her rosy cheeks to be most becoming. He cocked his head and raised an eyebrow, which only served to deepen the color in her cheeks. He grinned and turned his attention back to his paper.

He was quite looking forward to his lesson that afternoon. Despite his usual aversion to dancing, there were traits about the pastime he most certainly found appealing. For one thing, he was sure to have Kate's undivided attention for however long it took. And he was quite sure it would take a long time. For another, he was sure there would be a lot of touching going on. In addition to the steps of the dance that required hand brushes or holding hands, she would have to guide him and instruct him about. He tried to smother his broad smile. And if he could con her into trying out the infamous waltz…well, that would just be the icing on the cake.

He would have cackled to himself if Kate had not been present, he was so giddy with anticipation. He struggled to keep his excitement contained so Kate would not suspect his thoughts.

They finished up their breakfast fairly quickly. Kate was ready to get on with her day and accomplish all she had set out to do, and Nathaniel was always ready for a ride, especially when he knew he was going to be tucked away in his study for the majority of the day.

They separated to change into their riding gear and met up outside the stables, where their mounts were saddled and waiting for them. They traveled a different path than the day before. It was one they often traversed during their morning rides, and the familiarity of the route lent itself to discussion as they rode.

Nathaniel plied his wife as to her hopes for their ball, knowing it was a subject for which she had enthusiasm. He was not disappointed. She chattered animatedly about the topic for some time, only pausing to draw breath. He smiled at her fervor and hoped that hosting the ball would help her feel at home and invested in her future at Cheventhorpe.

When he mentioned the possibility of a new dress for the occasion, her eyes lit up. He knew she was conjuring up images of possible gowns in her mind as she rode.

"There is a modiste in Rotherham that I am told has an excellent reputation. Perhaps she might suffice for your needs?" Nathaniel suggested.

Kate agreed with his offer, loath to make the trip to Town and put herself in the crosshairs of the ton just for the purchase of a dress. She shuddered as she remembered the glares and giggles of her previous stay. She was glad to be sequestered at Cheventhorpe, away from the prying eyes and sharp tongues of the gentry. Cecelia might be convinced that her marriage would silence the gossip, but she was not so confident.

She refused to allow the painful memories of her time in Town interfere with her joy in hosting the ball. She decidedly turned her thoughts toward more pleasant things, namely the gown she was going to order.

Nathaniel had no interest in gown descriptions, but he encouraged her in her interest nonetheless. He may not care what style or fabrics she preferred, but he did want her to feel beautiful and look the part of Lady Rockingham. He would do all he could, and pay for all she desired, to make that happen. Because it was important to her, it would be important to him.

When they had looped back around and were headed back towards the stables, Kate looked over at him with a devil-may-care grin and urged her mare into a gallop. Nathaniel laughed at the silent taunt she cast over her shoulder at him and gave Abaccus his head.

This was no race. Their mounts were too well-matched for that. It was pure, unadulterated freedom; joy in motion. Abaccus matched his pace to Hera's. They were stride-for-stride, moving as one down the lane in a symphony of thundering hooves and labored breathing.

Nathaniel knew Kate's elation at the unrestraint of the moment. He knew her laughter and glee and the pure adrenaline that fueled their wild ride. Even more so, he knew the need to forget the burdens they carried as Lord and Lady Rockingham and to just be a man and a woman, young and carefree.

Kate reluctantly slowed Hera as they reached the end of the lane and Nathaniel reined in Abaccus beside her. His focus shifted as they neared the stables to the ledgers that waited for him in his study. There was much to be accomplished if he was going to be able to give his wife his full attention during their dance lesson.

Kate, too, was distracted as she pondered her visit with Mrs. Robinson. She had parted on good terms with the other woman, but a multitude of children in addition to being with child would wear on any woman. She hoped the visit would be a successful one.

They entered the stable yard and turned their horses over to the servants, parting as they entered the house.

*****

Alice Robinson was standing in the doorway, Henry balanced on one hip, as Kitty pulled into the yard. She waved a hand in greeting and shooed Tom out to take care of the ponies so Kitty could join her inside.

Kitty gathered up the basket by her feet that held her sewing things and went through the door Alice held open for her, stooping to bestow a kiss on Henry's chubby cheek as she did so. The little boy lurched forward in his mother's arms, reaching out his short arms in a bid for her attention. Kitty was only too happy to oblige. She laughed and scooped him out of Alice's grasp. The other woman gave him up willingly, stretching and rubbing away the ache in the small of her back as she was relieved of her burden.

They settled into the small sitting room at the front of the house and Alice pulled out the large basket of mending that resulted from a hard-working husband and five small children. She set the basket between them so it would be within easy reach of them both. Kitty set Henry down to play at her feet, needing both of her hands if she was to accomplish any good.

They both took an item of the clothing off the top and set to work. The conversation soon drifted toward the Robinson's children, and the unborn babe they were expecting in another month.

"I am most eager to meet this new little one," Alice commented, one hand resting protectively over her abdomen. "Sometimes I fear the delivery, but then I remember the joy of holding my babe in my arms and the fear just flits away."

Kate screwed up her face in distaste. "I was present when my friend Charlotte was delivered of a boy, and I must say it was a nerve-wracking experience. I thought the babe would never arrive. She toiled for over a day to bring him to birth."

Alice nodded sagely. "Aye. That must have been a very difficult delivery. My second, James, was like that. Still, there is the blessing of the child in the end."

Kitty remembered little William Collins and smiled wryly. "I am not so sure anyone in that household thought of him as a blessing. The babe came out wailing and did not stop for a full two weeks after his birth. There was very little sleep to be had."

Alice laughed. "There is never much sleep to be had with a new babe in the house, wailing or not. You will find that much out for yourself someday."

Kate smiled graciously, shifting uncomfortably at her words, and hurried to steer the conversation to safer grounds. "Have you settled on names yet for the babe?"

Alice was only too happy to tell her.

*****

When Kitty left, they had only made a small dent in the mending, but Alice was more than grateful for the help she had been able to lend. They made arrangements for her to return the following week, and then with a slap of the reins, she was off.

Nathaniel was watching for her return. His ledgers, despite their necessity, had not been enough to distract him completely. He had rushed through his work so that he would be done and ready whenever she returned.

He heard her quick steps on the stairs and their rapid tattoo as she passed the study door. He waited patiently, as he knew she would want to change before seeking him out. Finally, he heard her soft tread in the hall and he quickly busied himself with his papers.

The steps stopped outside his door and there was a brief pause before the door swung slowly open and she peeked around the corner.

"I have returned," she told him. "Have you finished?"

He closed the open ledger before him and stacked it on top of the book he had been entertaining himself with while he waited. "Yes, I am ready if you are." He rose and crossed the room to join her at the door.

He tucked her hand in his arm and laid his own tenderly on top before turning her to proceed down the hall. "Were you able to be of much assistance to Mrs. Robinson?"

"Some. It is difficult to accomplish anything with all those children running in and out of the room every few minutes. And the amount of mending that needs to be done is quite extraordinary. It was much too much for one sitting. But we were able to put a sizable dent in it, which is more than I think she expected. She seemed to be rather pleased with the progress, and therefore, I must be also."

"I am glad you were able to be of aid in the matter. The woman has quite enough on her plate to deal with without worrying about such trivial matters as the mending."

He guided her through the lengthy corridors to the empty ballroom. The room was large, ornate, and gilded. But it was designed for dancing, and since that was what he wanted to do, it was perfect for their purposes. Of course, it neglected to contain a pianoforte within its four walls, but since they had no one to play it for them, it was of no matter. When Cecelia returned to begin the plans for the ball he intended to enlist her assistance, but until then they would have to make do without music.

They decided to begin their practice with a lively country dance. With the absence of other dancers, this was quickly accomplished. Kitty found her husband to be light on his feet and he easily followed the rather simple steps of the dance.

She complimented him on his lightness of foot and he blushed. "You have not seen me try to perform the more complicated routines of the cotillion and the scotch reel yet."

He was right to be concerned, she found. When they attempted the more complex steps and patterns, he got hopelessly lost in the dance. He turned in the wrong direction, mixed up the steps, stepped on her toes, and almost clocked her in the nose with an unruly elbow. His dancing was not only unwieldy, it was downright dangerous!

She ordered him out of his shoes to protect her vulnerable toes, clad only in thin slippers, from his thick-soled boots. "Whatever are you doing wearing your boots inside?" Kate groused at him as he pulled them off and set them to one side. "You would do much better to have on your shoes or leather slippers when you are to be inside the whole of the day."

"I would prefer to be prepared, should my steward call me out for some business about the estate," Nathaniel replied shortly, already irritable and frustrated with himself.

Annoyance flashed across her face at his tone, but he ignored it, too wrapped up in his own exasperation to take notice of hers. This was not going as he had hoped. Instead of bringing them closer, it was beginning to be a source of contention.

They tried another set. This time a loose elbow made solid contact with her stomach as she went right and he went left.

Kate let out a loud, "Oof!" and doubled over as she had the wind knocked out of her.

Nathaniel was immediately horrified as to what he had done. He rushed to take her hands and inspect her face. "I am terribly sorry, my dear! Are you quite all right?"

Kate took several deep breaths before looking up into his face and smiling tremulously. "I think we had better try a different strategy."

He guided her to a bench set along the side of the room and sat her down to let her catch her breath. She rubbed her stomach gingerly where his blow had landed and willed the pain to lessen. It did, gradually. Nathaniel barely restrained himself from inspecting her stomach with his own hands to reassure himself she was truly alright.

He watched her carefully and breathed a sigh of relief when she removed her hand from its place against her abdomen. By now though, he was angry with himself.

He should never have put her in danger. He should have known he would run the risk of hurting her. His jaw tightened and his brow furrowed as he fought to keep his emotions under rigid control.

Kate noticed his tense features, and correctly surmised what was bothering him. She reached one hand over to smooth his brow and smiled tenderly. "You warned me you were not a good dancer," she told him gently. "This will be naught but a bruise tomorrow. Someday we may even look back on this and laugh. I will gladly endure a few bruises for the privilege of dancing with my husband."

She caressed his cheek and he lifted one hand to trap it, still against his skin. "I still do not like it," he said gruffly.

She smiled. "Then we shall do our best not to let it happen again." Her eyes lit mischievously. "I have been thinking of an analogy which might make things a little easier for you…" She proceeded to explain the connection she had thought of earlier between horseback riding and dancing.

A spark of understanding lit his eyes at her words. "Yes. I see what you mean." He stood and pulled her to her feet, his zeal renewed. "Come, let us try again."

They were much more successful this time around. He managed to keep his flailing limbs in check and avoided any further injuries to his partner. They were both smiling triumphantly at the end of the set.

Kate clapped her hands with excitement. "I knew you could do it! It is not so difficult after all."

Nathaniel was exultant, but not so easily reassured by his progress. "One set gone well could be a fluke. Let us go again."

They did, over and over, until the steps were branded into his memory and his feet could carry on without conscious thought on his part. The dinner bell was what eventually pulled them from their exercise.

They looked up in confusion at the sound of its ringing, having neglected to notice the lengthening shadows and the lateness of the hour.

They looked at each other, and Kate giggled. "I had not thought it so late."

He grinned and pulled her into an embrace. "The time certainly has passed quickly." He sat his chin on the top of her head as she rested her cheek against his chest. They stood there quietly for the space of several heartbeats before he added, "I know I am not an easy student, but you have been a very patient teacher with me."

She pulled back in his arms to grin up at him. "You *have* been a most difficult and, might I add, dangerous, pupil."

He groaned and tightened his hold on her. "Do not remind me."

She laughed at his discomfort. "I think that I must have some compensation for such a hazardous duty." She felt him chuckle.

"Must you?" he questioned good-naturedly. "Hmm…Well, then, what are your demands?"

She peeked up at him from her place in his arms. "A new fan and slippers to go with my gown for the ball?"

He smiled. "I think that can be arranged." He sighed and reluctantly released her from his grasp. She was just as disinclined to leave the warm circle of his arms, but she hid her disappointment well.

"We had better go change for dinner. Cook would not be pleased with us if we allowed his food to grow cold after all the effort he has put into preparing it."

*****

Their days took on a pattern after that. Cecelia returned as promised to begin the planning, and allowed herself to be persuaded into playing the pianoforte for them while they practiced dancing. She observed with pleasure their increased fondness for each other and the ease with which they got on. Their affection for one another was obvious, if not to them, at least to her.

The room rang with their laughter, and the servants would pause outside the door to listen to the joyful noise, reflecting with delight that it had been a long time since the house had been filled with such happiness.

In this way, a month passed quickly, and July was almost upon them.

CHAPTER THIRTEEN

The date of the ball was set for two weeks hence. The invitations had been sent out, Kate's gown had been ordered from the local modiste, and all their plans were set in motion. Kate was eagerly looking forward to it all.

Kate sat at the breakfast table, sipping her tea, pondering the bright morning and her desire to check on Alice. The other woman was very near to giving birth, and despite Alice promising to inform Kate as soon as the blessed event should occur, Kate worried. Should her labor start while her husband was still in the fields, she had naught but her children to help her. Only young Tom and James were old enough to be of any assistance, and only then to summon help. But the boys were often outside caring for chores, and out of earshot of their mother. Kitty chewed anxiously on her thumb.

She felt an innate urge to see her friend, just to make sure all was truly well. But Nathaniel had gone to Rotherham that morning to make some purchases, taking the phaeton and ponies she would have normally commandeered for her own use.

She could easily ride Hera, but she was loath to appear before her friend dressed in short pants and riding astride. There was nothing to be done for it. She would simply have to ride sidesaddle. Nathaniel had said Hera was broke for it, so there was little likelihood of there being any problems.

She pushed aside her nagging conscience. Surely Nathaniel had known there would be times it would be preferable she ride sidesaddle or he would not have purchased a mount for her that was broke for it. She tried to convince herself it was the truth, but there was a small nagging seed of doubt that refused to be ignored. Still, she was not about to let an officious statement by her husband stop her when the greater good was to be considered. She had Alice's welfare to think of here, not just her own. Surely, Nathaniel would not want her to sacrifice that just for the sake of a saddle!

She rose decidedly and went upstairs to change into her riding habit, instructing the butler to have Hera saddled and made ready for her to ride.

Half an hour later, she descended the stairs in her riding habit and collected Hera from the groom that was ready and waiting for her in the stable yard. By the time they made it out of the stable yard and on to the drive, it was obvious Hera was not happy with the change of riding style.

The mare snorted and tossed her head, flattening her ears angrily at the uneven weight.

Kitty could not say she was particularly happy about it either. She had quickly become accustomed to the ease of riding astride. It was much more difficult to remain balanced riding aside, and she had to remind herself to restrain Hera to a more sedate pace so as not to be unseated.

Kate kept a firm hand on the reins and a deep seat, struggling to keep her mount under control but refusing to allow Hera to win. Nathaniel had been right. A high-strung Thoroughbred was not well-suited to a sidesaddle.

Remarkably though, she made it to her destination unscathed. Young Tom was wide-eyed as he appeared around the corner to take her horse. She smiled at his obvious appreciation of the mare, but warned him that Hera could be a handful, especially as she was already disgruntled with the sidesaddle.

Tom regarded her seriously as she told him thus, and remained firmly planted by the mare's head while she went to knock on the door. Alice met her in the doorway.

"Have you come to check on me?" the young mother asked good-naturedly.

Kate smiled. "You know me too well."

Alice ushered her inside and seated her in the small sitting area before offering her some tea. Kitty declined, stating that she had only stopped for a brief visit before she needed to return to her own house. She had no desire to deplete the other woman's store of the precious commodity. Besides, she had to make it back before Nathaniel did, or she would be caught riding Hera aside.

Alice seemed to be in a particularly cheerful mood that morning. She chattered on for quite a while, filling Kate in on all she had been able to accomplish that week. Kate was impressed by the extensive list, and told her so.

Alice laughed. "This always happens right before the babe comes. I have this burst of energy and want to make sure everything is ready for the little one when it arrives."

Kate looked at her friend's swollen abdomen and puffy ankles and could not imagine wanting to do *anything* in that state, much less clean. She shrugged. To each their own.

They wrapped up their visit quickly after that, Kate fidgeting to get on her way back home, as Nathaniel was already sure to be hot on her heels. She collected Hera from Tom and turned the mare towards home.

They had just turned down the drive toward Cheventhorpe when it all went wrong.

A hare darted from the undergrowth beside the road in front of them. It startled them both, enough that Kate relaxed her grip on the reins for an instant. Hera, sensing her opportunity, reacted instantly, rearing up and taking the bit between her teeth as she came back down. She lunged forward, dragging the reins through Kate's fingers and taking off at a wild gallop down the lane. With the unstable sidesaddle, there was no way she could stay on at such an insane pace.

Kate felt herself falling and let go. She covered her face and head with her arms as she tumbled and took the brunt of the force of the fall on her left shoulder.

She sat up, dazed, in time to see Hera disappearing over the rise towards home. *At least I do not have to worry about trying to catch her*, Kitty thought. *She is headed straight for the stables.* Kitty sighed. *And with it, the servants.*

There would be no hiding her fall.

*****

Nathaniel was just handing over the phaeton and ponies when Hera came prancing into the stable yard, riderless and pleased with herself.

One of the grooms ran over to catch her reins and Nathaniel noted the sidesaddle on her back with alarm. He turned to the head groom, who was standing nearby. "Where is my wife?"

The man regarded him warily. "She took Hera out to pay a call on Mrs. Robinson."

Nathaniel felt like cursing the man for letting her go like that, but he bit back his anger. No servant would stand in the way of their mistress if she was determined to do something, no matter how foolhardy they may think it. "Get me Abaccus!" he snapped.

They had him tacked up and ready in record time.

Nathaniel threw himself into the saddle. "If I do not return with my wife in half an hour, I want every man in this household out on the grounds, searching for Lady Rockingham. Is that clear?" His gaze was cold and his voice threatening as he issued his commands.

The men gathered in the stable yard nodded mutely. They had never seen the master like this. They traded glances nervously as he swung his mount around and urged Abaccus out of the stable yard. The stallion could sense his master's urgency. Of his own initiative, the horse quickened his pace. Nathaniel smiled grimly. *That is it, old boy. Help me find her.*

Horse and rider moved as one as they raced down the lane. Nathaniel's heart pounded to the staccato cadence of Abaccus' hooves.

He crested a rise in the drive and saw a dirty and disheveled Kate picking her way towards him on foot. Immediately the tension and fear that had held his heart in its vise-like grip eased.

He was off Abaccus before his horse could come to a complete stop and took two large steps to close the distance that remained between him and his wife.

Kate eyed him hesitantly, unsure how he was going to react. Her back was stiff and her defenses up. He had obviously seen Hera and the sidesaddle. Would he be angry?

He pulled her into his arms and she relaxed against him for the space of two heartbeats as he held her there. Then he put her away from him so he could look her up and down and check for any injuries. "Are you quite alright?"

Kate smiled shakily. "A little bruised and battered, but not much worse for wear. I took the brunt of the fall on my shoulder."

Nathaniel resisted the urge to run his hands over her body and reassure himself of the truthfulness of her words. This was neither the time nor the place for such ministrations. "Can you move it?"

"Yes." She demonstrated, and winced at the pain.

Nathaniel's eyes softened at her distress and he gentled his touch. "It will no doubt be very sore, but it does not appear to be broken. We can be thankful for that much."

He walked with her to where Abaccus waited, grazing, and helped her into the saddle, mounting up behind her. He wrapped one strong arm around her midsection, holding her tightly to his chest as he guided Abaccus back down the drive towards home.

Kate knew the instant his relief turned to anger.

His body tensed, his grip on the reins tightened, and she did not have to turn around to know that his mouth was set in a firm, unyielding line. She was not surprised. Sooner or later, she had known he would comprehend that she had done the one thing he had expressly asked her not to do.

His fear for her safety had prevented those emotions from surfacing immediately, but now that the immediate danger had passed, they were present with a vengeance. She prepared herself for an onslaught, but it did not come.

They rode sedately back to the stable yard, where Nathaniel deposited Abaccus, and still he did not say a word. Together they entered the house and climbed the stairs to their quarters.

Kate stopped at her door and thanked him for his ministrations. He nodded mutely and reached around her to open her door, gesturing her inside. She did so, confused by his silence. To her surprise, he followed her in. She seated herself on the sofa at the foot of her bed and waited.

It was not until the door was firmly closed behind him that he unleashed his outrage.

He came to stand before her. His voice was deadly calm as he said, "I thought I particularly requested you to only ride Hera astride."

Kate tried to match his calm, preparing herself for the fury she knew lay beneath his cool demeanor. "You did."

"Then explain to me, please, how you came to be riding her sidesaddle." The words came out in a growl, his façade slipping as he lost control of his temper.

She sighed and stood, unwilling to allow him to tower over her. "I needed to check on Alice, as you very well know, and you had the phaeton and ponies. It was the most logical choice."

"You could have taken Luna, or waited for me to return! Or, if you were so determined to ride Hera, you could have gone astride!"

"*That* would hardly have been proper," she retorted sarcastically. "Think what the townsfolk would say if Lady Rockingham were to be spotted astride- in short pants no less!"

He took a step toward her. "I hardly think you need fear the consternation of mere villagers, *my Lady*."

She mimicked his stance and stepped closer, her own ire rising, until they were nose-to-nose. Her chest rose and fell in a huff of indignation. "I will not allow you to order me about as if I were a mere house servant! I have as fine a seat as you and if that stupid hare had not decided to cross our path, you would be none the wiser of my ride! I do not see why this is any of your concern!" She punctuated her words with a firm poke of her finger in the center of his chest.

He grabbed the offending digit and restrained her from repeating the gesture when she would have done so again. "You could have been hurt! Or worse! Which is exactly the reason why I forbid it in the first place!"

"You are the most arrogant, insufferable man! To think you have the audacity to tell me what to do-!" She stomped her foot and whirled away from him.

"And you are the most stubborn, petulant *child* of my acquaintance!" He stormed across the room to stand rigidly by the door. "You have said quite enough, madam! I perfectly comprehend your feelings. I shall leave you to yourself!" He flung open the door and disappeared through it, slamming it so fiercely behind him that the thud echoed through the hallway and surrounding rooms.

Kate winced at the noise and sank gratefully on to the sofa as all the fight drained out of her.

*****

Nathaniel stormed out of the house and into the stable yard. The servants fled from before his thunderous visage, but he found his quarry easily enough. "I want Abaccus brought round," he snapped at the head groom.

The man met his gaze steadily, when he should have been quaking in his boots, irritating Nathaniel further. Did no one in this household recognize he was the master here? Had they no respect for his authority? He ground his teeth together and clenched his jaw.

"Yes, my Lord," the man said evenly, and moved off to see about taking care of it.

Nathaniel waited impatiently for his horse to be brought round, pacing in the stable yard. He heard the staff whispering among themselves as they gave him a wide berth in order to go about their duties.

When the head groomsman finally brought round Abaccus, he had worked himself into even more of a tizzy. He grabbed the reins from the man without a word of thanks and swung up on the stallion. He whirled him round to race recklessly out of the yard and down the lane.

*****

Kate repaired to her sitting room soon after Nathaniel had stormed out of her room. She desired peace and solitude to sort out her feelings and knew it was the one room in the house she was least likely to be disturbed in. The cozy chamber welcomed her and embraced her with its warmth.

She wished desperately for a cup of tea to settle her nerves, but was too embarrassed to appear before any of the servants and request it after such a terrible row. Surely they must have heard them arguing.

She raised trembling hands to her hot cheeks, mortified at her behavior. She should never have allowed Nathaniel to bait her so. Ladies did not shout or stomp their feet when they were upset. They faced the world with equanimity, despite how others might incite them to act otherwise.

He was wrong to think he could order her about, but she had been wrong to disregard such a paltry request. He was right; she very easily could have ridden the much more even-tempered Luna. But she had stubbornly chosen to do things her own way without a thought for the consequences. She shuddered now to think of what could have happened. She was fortunate, indeed, to have come away from the incident with only a sore shoulder.

She was wrenched from her ruminations by a knock on the sitting room door. She sighed heavily and rose to answer the knock.

Fanny stood wide-eyed and hesitant on the other side of the door. She shifted uneasily from foot to foot. "Begging yer pardon, ma'am, but there's a message for ya from Mrs. Robinson."

Kitty read the hastily scrawled note Fanny handed her. She frowned. Her own troubles with her husband would have to wait. "Is Tom is still below stairs?"

"He is. Cook was plying him with some sweets as I left."

"Good. See to it he is given a little something to eat and then have the phaeton brought round in about twenty minutes. Mrs. Robinson has gone into labor and it seems the good doctor has been held up at the Milbanks. She has asked for my assistance, and I shall not deny her." Kate spoke briskly, her mind already shifting focus to the long night ahead.

Fanny curtsied and disappeared to do her bidding. Kate sighed and went to root about in her wardrobe for an old dress to change into and an apron to go over it. She rounded up a few other odds and ends she knew might be useful in the birthing room and then descended the stairs to find her phaeton and young Tom waiting for her, as requested.

She hid her smile at the remnants of chocolate that rimmed the little boy's mouth and instead thanked him seriously for delivering his mother's message so quickly.

His chest puffed up with pride at her praise and only swelled further when she suggested he take the ribbons of the phaeton.

She smiled at his enthusiasm and made sure he had a firm grasp of the basics of driving before she allowed her mind to wander to what awaited her at the Robinsons.

*****

Nathaniel rode furiously. He gave Abaccus his head, surging forward with no clear destination in mind. He did not want to think or reason. He was too angry with Kate to think clearly. He wanted to yell, or throw things, or hit something. But instead he released his pent up frustration and anger into the vigorous ride.

Stupid, stupid, girl, he thought angrily, his mind whirling in circles. *She could have been killed!* The thought only fueled his fury, and he urged Abaccus faster, his unseeing eyes failing to note the changing terrain as they neared the woodlands.

The stallion responded gamely to his urgings, dredging up even more speed from whatever reserves he had left. They entered the tree line on a seldom used path. The forest undergrowth had started to creep inwards in some areas, narrowing the path until it was barely wide enough for a horse and rider.

None of this gave Nathaniel any pause, as he was far too absorbed in his own thoughts to give consideration to anything else. He was snapped out of his stupor though, when Abaccus ducked his head to avoid a low-hanging branch.

Even Nathaniel's quick reflexes were not quick enough. He had no time to prepare himself, no time to react. The branch caught him solidly across the chest, sweeping him off his mount. His right ankle caught briefly in his stirrup, wrenching painfully before coming free. He fell with a thud, absently aware of Abaccus careening forward through the undergrowth as he tumbled.

And then everything went black as his head hit the ground.

CHAPTER FOURTEEN

Darkness had long since fallen when Kate finally arrived home, exhausted and weary to the core. Alice had been delivered of a healthy baby girl, the doctor arriving just in time to oversee the birth.

She smiled as she remembered Edmond Robinson's frantic pacing outside of his wife's door, and the relief on his face at the newborn's lusty cries. When she had finally ushered him inside to meet his daughter, the look of tenderness and love that passed between husband and wife had made her step outside, a lump in her throat.

She was looking forward to telling Nathaniel about the new babe, Sarah, named after Edmond's sister. Surely, by now he would have forgiven her, or at least cooled down some.

One of the servants came out to take the ponies, and she gratefully accepted a hand out of the phaeton. She stepped down and paused to stretch her back after the drive back. A normally easy drive during the day had proved to be a tense ride back in the dark. It had been difficult to see, the moon hidden behind dense clouds. A flash of lightning in the distance caught her eye, and a rush of relief washed over to have made it home before the storm hit.

She went slowly up the steps, half expecting her husband to come out to meet her, only to be greeted at the door by Mrs. Davis. She took one look at the woman's expression and instantly knew something was gravely wrong.

"What has happened, Mrs. Davis?"

The older woman wrung her hands. "The master went out for a ride before you left to attend Mrs. Robinson, and he has yet to return. I fear something terrible must have happened to him." Her eyes filled up with tears and a guilty conscience.

Kate rested one hand reassuringly on the housekeeper's shoulder and tried to answer her calmly, despite her own rising fear. "Have you sent out a search party?"

Mrs. Davis nodded. "When darkness fell and he still had not returned we grew worried and some of the men have gone out to look for him."

"Has Abaccus returned without him?"

Mrs. Davis shook her head mutely.

Kate frowned. That could either be good or bad. On the one hand, Nathaniel could still be out riding, working off some steam on Abaccus. Or it could mean that some sort of trouble had befallen them both.

She rubbed a weary hand across her tired eyes. "Please have Luna saddled and brought round for me. I am going to change into my riding gear and then join the search party." She stayed Mrs. Davis with one hand as the other woman would have moved off. "Please do not blame yourself, Mrs. Davis. You have done exactly as you should have in this situation. No one could expect any more."

The relief on the housekeeper's face was immediate. Kate shook her head as she trudged up the stairs. As if she would blame her for Nathaniel's actions, rushing off headlong like that.

She hoped that by the time she had changed and come back down, the search party would have returned, their quarry found. But it was not so.

As she mounted Luna, the night sky lit overhead with a flash of lightning and sounded with a deafening crash of thunder.

Fear knotted her gut. This was not a good night to be out in. She took the lantern Mrs. Davis offered her mutely, and spurred Luna into motion.

She had no idea where to look.

*****

When Nathaniel woke, it was dark. Disoriented and dazed, he lay there, trying to make sense of it all when a soft whiffing in his ear drew him out of his haze.

Abaccus stood over him, nudging him gently with his muzzle and blowing into his ear. Nathaniel found it to be a little disconcerting to have the large animal so close and pushed his head away. "Yes, yes, old boy. I am alive. Now give me some room to breathe."

Abaccus obligingly took a few steps back and fell to grazing on the undergrowth. Nathaniel attempted to sit up, finding the endeavor hampered by the spinning in his head. He groaned and laid his head on his arms as he waited for the sensation to ease.

When it finally did, a good several minutes later, he tried to take stock of himself. He felt his head with one hand, and flinched when he touched a tender spot. He must have hit his head when he had been knocked off.

His head clearing, he suddenly became aware of an intense throbbing in his ankle. He remembered with sudden clarity his foot getting stuck in the stirrup as he fell, and groaned. He tried to rotate his ankle to test it, and stifled a cry of pain. It was no doubt sprained, and there was no way he would be able to trek all the way back to the house on it. In fact, he very much doubted he would be able to put any weight on it at all.

Thunder rumbled, close overhead, and with sudden horror, Nathaniel noticed the approaching storm. There was a charge in the air. Lightning crackled above him and thunder shook the ground at almost the same moment. Any second now, the skies were going to open up and he would be drenched.

He looked about him for a suitable shelter, but there was none. Instead, he managed to drag himself and maneuver so his back was against the trunk of a nearby tree. Abaccus joined him under its sheltering branches, his head down and facing out.

No one would be out in this storm to rescue him. He thought ruefully of Kate and their quarrel that afternoon. She had every right leaving him out in the rain to cool off. He was chagrined to admit that he was guilty of the exact same transgressions he had accused her of that morning, with far more disastrous consequences. He had been riding without a thought for his own safety, overconfident in his abilities as a horseman. What a fine mess he had gotten himself into.

He huddled closer against the tree as the rain began to fall. It was going to be a miserable night.

*****

Kitty rode unrelentingly through the storm. The rain mingled with the tears that streamed down her cheeks, soaking her to the core. *Where was Nathaniel?* Lightning briefly lit the path ahead and she hungrily sought for any sign of his presence. Once more, she was disappointed.

Her heart ached with the realization that he was in danger. Her husband would never purposefully stay out in weather like this. Something must have gone terribly wrong. She sniffled and wiped the back of her hand across her eyes.

He had to be alright! He just had to! She would never be able to live with herself if he was not. She pressed forward, trying to ignore the storm around her and the ache in her injured shoulder, earnestly peering about for any clue that might lead her to him, even as the rain did its best to wash them all away. She despaired of ever finding him, and yet could not bear to return without him.

He would be so angry if he knew I was out here in the storm searching for him. She smiled at the thought. She would gladly risk his wrath if she could just find the man!

She turned Luna further into the tree line to get some shelter from the downpour. *Not that it would make much of a difference*, she thought wryly, *I am already drenched.*

Her lantern cast shadows off the tree branches dancing wildly in the wind. Luna flicked her ears forward curiously, but plodded on. Kate was grateful for the foresight that had made her request Luna. The mare was far more even-tempered than Hera, and had proven her worth in the storm. She was certain if she had been on Hera the mare would have thrown her by now and high-tailed it back to her stall. She had already displayed her dislike for storms on the day of their picnic.

Luna suddenly lifted her head, pausing to listen intently. Then with a joyful whinny she took off, plowing through the underbrush without waiting for direction from Kate. Unsettled by the uncharacteristically fast pace from the lethargic mare, Kate endured several hard bounces before she found her seat.

An answering whinny drifted on the wind from the heading Luna had set them on. Kate's mouth dropped open at the sound. There could be no mistaking that noise. It was Abaccus, and he sounded very pleased to hear Luna.

Kate's heart leapt in her throat, and then took off, racing with anticipation. Just ahead, she could make out Abaccus, watching eagerly for them to appear. She cast the lantern around, looking for any sign of Nathaniel, and finally spotted him, pressed tightly against the tree trunk, eyes closed and deathly pale. Her heart hammered in her chest as she slid off Luna and ran to fall at his side, fearing the worst.

She put one trembling hand to his cheek and shook his shoulder gently with the other. "Nathaniel?"

Kitty wept with relief when he opened sleepy eyes and peered at her in confusion.

*****

Nathaniel blinked. Surely he must be dreaming. There was no way Kate would be out on such a dangerous night. Yet, the concerned face hovering above his certainly *seemed* real and those cold hands that were exploring his limbs, checking for broken bones, *definitely* felt real. The pain they incited when they reached his swollen ankle was explosive enough to shake him out of his stupor and convince him he was not dreaming.

He bit his lip to keep from crying out, but could not stop the groan that welled up from the pain of her gentle touch. He looked up and met his wife's panicked eyes.

"Stop poking and prodding, Kate," he grumbled. "I am perfectly alright except for a nasty bump on the head and a sprained ankle."

The relief in her eyes was immediate. She threw her arms around him and buried her face in the side of his neck. "You stupid, stupid man! How could you do that to me?!"

Nathaniel shifted gingerly, careful of his ankle, to wrap his arm around her. "I did not fall off on purpose, you know." He started suddenly, realizing she was sobbing against his neck. He patted her back awkwardly. "There,

there, dear. I really am fine. There is no cause for you to weep."

She sat back on her heels and brushed the moisture from her cheeks. "If you had not raced off like that, I would not be! When I found out you were lost somewhere in the storm-" She cut herself off and shook her head. "I was scared to death I had lost you."

Nathaniel quirked up one corner of his mouth. "I would think you would be glad to get rid of an old codger like me."

Kate smacked his shoulder. "How could you say something like that!" She sniffled and turned away from him, suddenly shy. "No, you old fool, I love you."

Nathaniel sat stock still for several moments, processing her words, afraid to believe his ears. Then a radiant grin broke over his face. He tried to tamp down the joy that threatened to overpower him. He had to know exactly what she meant by that. He reached out gentle hands to turn his wife to face him.

She refused to meet his eyes, so he took one finger and gently tilted her chin upward until her gaze met his. "Do you mean that in the way I think you do?"

She bit her lip and cast her gaze back down before peeking up at him through her lashes. She did not have to answer. He could see her reply shining in her eyes. But she did anyway, reluctantly. "I do."

Nathaniel gathered her into his arms, forgetting completely about his injured foot. "Well then. We might have to do something about that." Their gazes caught and held before his gaze flicked to her mouth and settled on her lips. The air hummed between them, fraught with anticipation. Kitty sucked in a breath as she realized what his intentions were. He lowered his head and pressed his lips tenderly against hers.

Their first kiss was everything a first kiss should be. Tender and sweet, full of hope and promise for the future. Neither of them ever wanted it to end. When Nathaniel finally did pull away, it was to lean his head against hers and smile lovingly at her.

"Oh Kate, I love you, too."

CHAPTER FIFTEEN

Under normal circumstances, such declarations of love would have as a matter of course been followed by numerous assurances and expressions of affection. But these were no ordinary circumstances, and the inclement weather soon intruded on the two lovers.

As reluctant as they were to part, they agreed that it would be best for all involved if they were to head in, out of the storm.

Kate helped Nathaniel to his feet, holding him steady until the spinning in his head stopped. He was forced to lean on her good shoulder to support himself as she helped him to hobble to Abaccus' side. He was apologetic for the necessity, but she bore up well under his weight and refused to allow him to feel guilty, as much as he would have liked to.

With her assistance, he was able to mount awkwardly. Concerned about his lingering dizziness, Kate confiscated his reins and led Abaccus behind her.

By the time they made it back to the house, the storm had eased to a constant drizzle. Regardless, they were soaked through when they appeared in the stable yard. Servants came rushing forward in relief to collect their mounts.

Kate slid off Luna and let one of the stable hands quickly lead her away. She hurried to help Nathaniel, who was still perched precariously on Abaccus. She reached up reassuring hands to steady him and called over a particularly burly groom.

"Careful!" she warned, as he moved to assist Nathaniel off his horse. "He is hurt! His ankle is badly sprained and he has had quite a knock to the head." The man gentled his touch, cautiously maneuvering around his ankle until Nathaniel was back on level ground.

Kate followed behind as the servant helped Nathaniel into the house, wringing her hands and wishing she could be the one he was leaning on. She knew that Nathaniel would prefer not to burden her with his weight. She smiled. It was in his nature to protect and care for her, and he was uncomfortable to have the role reversed.

Mrs. Davis met them at the door with blankets, shaking her head over their condition. Kate let the men begin the climb upstairs, knowing that it was a long and arduous journey to Nathaniel's chambers, up the stairs and down the never ending maze of halls. She lingered behind to speak with the housekeeper.

"I sent for the doctor as soon as I was informed you had returned," Mrs. Davis informed her.

Kate nodded and responded gratefully, "Thank you. I am glad to hear that. Please inform me when he arrives so that I may speak to him before he goes in to Nathaniel."

The housekeeper assured her that she would do so and Kate made her own way to her chambers. Fanny quickly helped her out of her wet clothes and into something suitable to receive the doctor in. There was no time to dry her hair by the fire, so Kate simply removed the few pins that had managed to stay in and let it tumble down her back, hoping it would air dry some before the doctor arrived.

She dismissed Fanny and went to knock nervously on the connecting door, holding her breath until Nathaniel called out from the other side. She opened the door and peeked in, hesitant lest she should catch him in a state of undress.

He was propped up in bed, his valet having helped him to change into his nightclothes. The man discreetly disappeared into the adjoining dressing room upon her arrival, remaining near in case his master should need him, while affording them the privacy they so desired.

She came to perch on the side of his bed, eagerly taking the hands he held out to her. "How are you feeling, my love?"

Nathaniel smiled at the endearment and squeezed her hands. "Much better, now that we are both safely ensconced at home."

"I am glad to hear that, for the doctor has been sent for, and he is sure to make you uncomfortable once again very shortly," she teased.

Nathaniel groaned. "Surely I have been through enough misery for one day!"

She laughed at the twinkle in his eye. "Just a little bit more to ensure you are set to rights."

"I suppose I shall be made to bear up and endure." He cocked his head and surveyed her. "I was informed that you had a very eventful day as well."

She smiled brilliantly at the reminder of little Sarah's birth. It seemed an eternity ago now, having spent heart-rending hours searching for Nathaniel in the rain. There was much to be thankful for this day.

A knock sounded at the door and Kate rose gracefully to answer it. "That is a story for another time, I am afraid." She conferred briefly with someone at the door, and then turned to inform Nathaniel, "The doctor has arrived. I am just going to go down to speak with him briefly, and then I shall bring him up."

Nathaniel waited impatiently for her to return. Having informed the good doctor of the condition in which she had found her husband and any further observations she had made as to his health, she brought the man up to make his examination.

She retreated to the armchair by the window, where she had so long ago caught him engrossed deeply in his book, and laid her head back against the chair as the doctor went about his business. The adrenaline rush that had carried her through the hours of searching and the long ride back was fading fast.

It had been an exhausting day, and the effects of it were quickly catching up with her. The warmth of the room seeped into her weary bones and the armchair wrapped her in its snug embrace. Her eyelids grew heavy and her mouth stretched into a wide yawn as the doctor's voice droned in the background. *I will just close my eyes for a moment,* she thought. It was the last conscious thought she had.

*****

The doctor seemed, to Nathaniel's reckoning at least, to take an interminably long time with his examination. He was anxious to be left alone with his wife, and the man seemed to be in no hurry at all, twisting his ankle into any excruciatingly painful direction he could.

Finally, the man seemed satisfied with his work and stepped back to make some notations and dig about in his bag. Nathaniel gritted his teeth in irritation and tried to dredge up the last vestiges of his patience.

The doctor gave his diagnosis, a sprained ankle, and prescribed rest and elevation of the foot, with laudanum for the pain if necessary. Nathaniel was glad to see the back of the man as he departed and quickly dismissed his valet afterwards.

He turned his gaze to the chair his wife occupied by the window and immediately his gaze softened. She had fallen asleep, her head propped on one hand. Her cheeks were flushed with sleep and her mane of unruly chestnut curls cascaded over one shoulder in wild abandon.

He debated briefly whether to wake her or not, she looked so peaceful. But he knew if he did not she would wake with a stiff neck some time later. There was no way she could sleep the night through in that position. He called her name quietly, hoping she was not so deeply asleep he would be unable to wake her without getting out of bed. He really did not want to be on his ankle anymore that night.

She stirred at the sound of his voice, albeit reluctantly. He smiled tenderly at the frown that marred her delicate features and the twin lines that furrowed her brow. Her eyes did not open.

"Kate," he called again. "The doctor has gone and if you remain in that position you shall regret it."

Grudgingly, her eyes flickered open and he grinned widely at the glare of utter petulance she gave him.

He held a hand out to her and invited her to join him on the bed. "Come, my dear. You shall be much more comfortable up here with me."

He was gratified when she unfurled herself from the chair and climbed in next to him. She curled against his side, resting her head on his chest, and he settled his arm around her, relishing the warmth of her body against his.

It did not take long for her body to relax again in sleep. Nathaniel stared up at the ceiling, a small smile playing about his lips as his wife slept beside him. He was sure he would get no sleep that night, but it was all worth it.

Finally, things were the way they were meant to be between them. All the misunderstandings had been cleared up. His wife loved him. And he loved her.

Kate was where she was supposed to be, beside him, in his arms, sharing his life. He looked forward to the opportunity to wake up beside her every morning and fall asleep beside her every night.

They still had some hurdles to overcome, but the largest one had been crossed that night.

CHAPTER SIXTEEN

The day of a ball is always one of excitement and anticipation for any young lady, but it was especially so on this day for Kitty. With the usual anxieties of gowns and gloves and hair, came the additional stresses of hosting the ball. Kate was grateful for her competent staff, who, despite the lack of festivities in recent years at Cheventhorpe, were well equipped for the challenge. Mrs. Davis ran a tight ship, and it was with a relatively easy mind that Kitty was able to leave the preparations to the housekeeper and take herself upstairs to dress.

The household was bustling with activity all around her, but her chambers were a calm amidst the storm. She and Fanny chatted away amicably as Fanny styled her hair. For once, her disorderly tresses submitted meekly to the maid's ministrations. There was not a strand out of place as Fanny helped her into her emerald gown and draped a simple diamond pendant around her neck.

Kate stood for a long time in front of the looking glass, admiring her reflection. She looked and felt like a true lady for the first time that night. She had grown into her role as

Marchioness. She would never be the proud, stern, regal woman she had first associated with the role, but that was never who she had wanted to become anyway. She laughed, and rode astride, and raced with her husband. But she also cared deeply for the people who were under her protection. She was willing to go out of her way to help them if she could. And that made her far more of a true lady than many of the other peers of the realm.

A soft knock on the door interrupted her thoughts. She turned to smile at her husband as he peeked his head around the door.

"Are you ready?" he asked. Seeing she was, he grinned broadly at the sight of her, and came into the room, leaving the door open behind him. "You look especially lovely tonight, my love."

She smiled radiantly and came to take the hands he held out to her. "And you look especially handsome, my husband."

He encouraged her to twirl for him, so that he might admire her gown, specially commissioned for the occasion, from every angle.

After every suitable exclamation and assurance as to the gown's perfection, and the perfection of the woman it encased, had been made, Nathaniel suggested they descend to inspect the arrangements and prepare for the arrival of their guests.

Kate was overawed by the magnificence of the ballroom as they entered the space. It was the first time she had seen it opened and lit. The room was two stories high, with marble columns around the outskirts of the room supporting a balcony above the main dance floor. The marble floors gleamed from the light of the candelabras and the grand crystal chandelier that hung prominently from the center of the tray ceiling. The heady scent of the numerous floral arrangements filled the space with a pleasant aroma.

Kate stood in the center of the room, on her husband's arm, taking it all in. "I do not think I have ever seen a more beautiful, or well-appointed, room."

Nathaniel laughed at her statement but could not help but agree with her. "It is a spectacular sight when it is done up like this. It is a shame it has been closed up for so many years." He wrapped an arm around her waist and pulled her against his side. "You are bringing life back into this old house."

Kate shook her head. "*We* are bringing life back into it. One of these days I want to be able to look at this cavernous place and see it as a home, not just a house."

Nathaniel looked down lovingly at his wife. "It is getting closer every day that you are here."

Kate smiled back up at him tenderly, reaching a hand up to caress his cheek. "You give me far too much credit."

They were interrupted by the butler clearing his throat in the doorway. "Excuse me, my Lord and my Lady," he intoned, "but may I suggest you take your place in the entryway to receive your guests?"

The couple shared a smile at his solemn visage and moved to the entryway to meet their guests.

It was a wonderful evening, full of light and love and hope. There could be no doubt among those that attended that their hosts had finally admitted the love the neighborhood had known was there all along. Nathaniel and Kate were never far from each other's side, whether it was on the dance floor, or at dinner, or just simply chatting with their visitors. They shared secret, loving smiles over their punch glasses and often had to be recalled to the conversation by their companions as they displayed an innate tendency to stare dreamily into space.

Their guests bore all this with a fond forbearance.

And when the night was over, and the guests had all left in the hazy light of dawn, the Marquess of Rockingham collapsed in an armchair and pulled his giggling wife into his lap.

"Well, my dear," he said. "I believe that was an unequivocal success."

She giggled and laid her weary head against his. "I think I must agree."

"I must say, that was the most enjoyable ball I have ever attended. And I have suffered through my fair share of them."

Kate smiled up at him. "That is because you had a most pleasant partner instead of being forced to suffer through an endless line of debutantes."

Nathaniel answered her lightly, "Hmmm… Yes, I think there are some definite benefits to this whole marriage thing."

Kate responded with mock irritation, "I should hope you would think so!"

Nathaniel sobered. "I would never have dreamed it to be so, when it happened, but I find myself quite glad I accidently compromised you back in Kent. Mr. Collins could not have known how happy he would make me. I cannot imagine how dreary my life would be without you in it."

Kate stroked his cheek tenderly. "I would never have suspected that such a horrid day would turn out to be the source of such joy." She crinkled her nose. "Especially after you had so summarily dismissed me as uninteresting the night before."

Nathaniel was stricken. "You overheard my conversation with Colonel Fitzwilliam?"

"Yes, you dolt. My hearing is perfectly well, and I was not so far away from you."

He blushed. "I thought…" He faltered, then continued, "Never mind. What you should know is that I was utterly bewitched by you when I saw you outside the parsonage. But then when you appeared at Rosings Park, you were so subdued…"

"I had a dreadful headache! The Collins' babe would not stop its screaming, day or night!"

Nathaniel laughed at her righteous indignation. "I daresay no one would be at their best under the circumstances. And to own the truth, I was rather irked myself to be stuck in the company of Lady Catherine and her pompous clergyman, when I should have rather spent it with Colonel Fitzwilliam. Do say you will forgive me, love, for the awful way I acted?"

She pretended to consider his words. "I suppose I shall if you will forgive all the awful things I thought about you."

He laughed and tightened his arms around her. "I think I shall be able to. And just to prove there is no ill will…" He leaned forward to close the small gap that remained between them and pressed a lingering kiss to her waiting lips.

She wound her arms around his neck and leaned back with a sigh of contentment when he finally broke their kiss. "I may be an unlikely marchioness," she said. "But I am certainly the happiest."

Nathaniel could not help but agree.

EPILOGUE

Nathaniel had lost his wife. He had already searched all through the house, to no avail. He was far too proud to resort to asking one of the many servants, who bustled about briskly, but he was reasonably certain she could not have wandered far, limited as she was at the moment in her modes of transportation.

There was only one place left to check. He made his way nonchalantly to the stables, whistling lightly under his breath as he went.

He smiled as he rounded a corner in the building and heard Kate's voice, drifting to him on the breeze. His gaze softened as he caught sight of her, perched on a hay bale outside of Hera's stall. Her beauty never ceased to amaze him. His eyes drifted to her rounded belly, where their child grew, and he smiled as he thought of the life that was soon to join them.

"I see you have been talking to the old girl again." The mare had her head over the barrier, listening intently to whatever Kate had been saying.

Kate smiled as he came to join her on the bale. "Hera is not old, are you girl?"

The mare snorted and shook her head, drawing a giggle from Kate.

"Very well," Nathaniel said. "I retract my comment. What have you been talking about?"

Kate laid one hand on her expanding stomach and sighed. "Oh, just complaining, one mother to another."

Nathaniel nodded sympathetically. His free-spirited wife was not used to being confined to the house and its immediate grounds. But even worse to her, it had been months since she had been able to indulge in a horseback ride. The danger to their unborn child was too great for her to go gallivanting around the countryside as she was used to. He knew she missed the independence and joy riding gave her.

Wisely, he held his tongue. Kate sighed again and went on grumpily. "I do wish this little one would join us soon. I am quite tired of waiting, and I do not think it would be possible for me to grow any rounder."

Nathaniel struggled not to laugh. "I think you grow more and more beautiful every day."

She rolled her eyes. "You would not say that if you were in my position. I look like a toad."

Nathaniel wrapped his arm around her waist and tugged her closer. She laid her head on his shoulder. "Every time I look at you I see the same carefree, vivacious woman that so captured my attention outside the parsonage in Kent."

Kate smiled up at him and admitted, "You always know just the thing I need to hear, even in the most trying of circumstances."

Their babe chose that moment to give his mother a resounding kick in the ribs. Kate groaned, while Nathaniel avidly watched her stomach for any further movement. Kate smiled at his piqued interest and invited him to lay his hand on her belly, lest he should miss feeling the next time their child kicked.

The picture they thus presented, to all those so fortunate as to observe it, was one of familial bliss. It was not always to be so, as the years passed. The couple, as any does, had their differences. Two such passionate and vivacious people cannot by necessity always agree. But the lessons learned early in their marriage on the vitality of communication stood them in good stead, and they were always able to settle their differences satisfactorily.

As their family grew, so did their love. Once more, Cheventhorpe was filled was light and laughter. Children's voices rang through the once empty halls and little feet ran lithely down its stairs. There were many races down the banisters in the front entry and games of hide-and-seek in the countless rooms.

The foal Hera bore was the start of a line of great racehorses born in Cheventhorpe's stables. Their spirited mounts came to be coveted the world over for their strength, stamina, and character.

The realization of their dreams was only a small part of their life together. Together, they turned a house into a home. And together, they built a family that laughed and loved... *and lived.*

**Don't miss the next book by
Lelia M. Silver!**

An Unexpected Governess

PROLOGUE

It all started with a letter. One heart-wrenching, tear-jerking, earth-shattering letter. In the space of a moment, of a sentence, everything changed. Thomas Bowen's life would never be the same.

That letter was the reason he had left his comfortable home in Hertfordshire and journeyed to Portsmouth. Now, he stood high on Portsdown Hill, overlooking the town and harbor below. The gray skies matched his dull mood and the town spread before him was dingy and repulsive in comparison to the bright fields he had traveled from. It was hardly welcoming. He hesitated to descend into the town itself, afraid of what waited for him below.

He knew in the end he would, as it was expected of him, and he could hardly forsake the responsibility that awaited him. But still he dawdled, turning his hat round and round in his hands as the skies threatened to open up on him.

He was not normally a man of inaction. His estate, Kaverstow, had flourished under his competent guidance. But he was a man used to his own company and his own comforts, without the distractions of a family.

He led a carefully ordered life. Breakfast was served precisely at 8:00 a.m., and dinner at 6:00 p.m. He spent his days either in his study with his ledgers or with his steward in the fields. In the evenings, he entertained himself with a book before a warm fire. He very rarely attended any social functions, as he found them quite tedious and taxing. His retiring nature and awkward manners were not well-suited to the ballroom or parlor.

Still, he was quite pleased with his life. It suited him just fine the way things were. It was the knowledge that all this was about to change that frightened him.

No member of his household would dare to upset his sensibly orchestrated existence. He chewed anxiously on his bottom lip. But it was not the current members of his household he was worried about. His home was about to be invaded by four small strangers, and he had no doubt that his comfortable life was about to be turned upside down.

It was sad, really, that they were strangers. He had been very fond of his younger sister before she had married a navy man and moved to Portsmouth. He had intended to visit her, of course, but somehow Kaverstow had always occupied his time, and Anne had been far too busy running her little household in her husband's absence to travel to Hertfordshire.

They had taken for granted that they had all the time in the world to close the distance that had gaped between them. He sighed. And now it was too late.

Anne was gone, and he would never have the chance to see her, settled in her home, proud of her efficiently run household, with her children gathered around her and her beloved husband nearby.

He would have preferred that his nieces and nephew had known him before now. It would make things infinitely easier. As it was, they would no more recognize him than he would them. And he had come to take them away from the only home they had ever known.

He sighed again and replaced his hat on his head as rain began to drizzle from the sky. It was a thankless task he had to do, but he had best be on with it.

CHAPTER ONE

A man could only take so much squealing.

Thomas was positive the noise level was going to drive him to insanity before he was thirty. He would never have believed little girls could be *so loud*. His carefully managed household had disintegrated into chaos in the past month.

There were stains on the dining room chairs where the children had spilled their food when he had mistakenly believed they could all sit round the table for a family meal. He had learned his lesson with that one. Now, they took their meals in the nursery. The four of them ran roughshod over the house, sliding down banisters and climbing the curtains. On the bright side, his banisters never needed polishing. But his curtains were in tatters.

So were his nerves.

He was looking forward with unbridled and unusual glee to a visit to his attorney that morning, a Mr. Phillips in Meryton. How he longed for adult conversation! To be somewhere quiet and peaceful! To complete a discussion without interruption!

It was all very much to be longed for and looked forward to with the greatest of expectations.

The door burst open and two little girls, followed closely by their brother, ran into his study.

"Uncle Thomas! Uncle Thomas! John pulled my hair!"

"I did not! You are lying!"

"Did too!"

"Did not!"

"Did too!"

Thomas rubbed his temples. Yes, a visit to the attorney was definitely in order. He was past ready to escape this madhouse for some civilized company!

*****

Mr. Philips was shocked speechless when the normally staid Thomas Bowen entered his office whistling merrily. He had never seen the man so at ease. He actually *lounged* in the armchair across from him.

He raised his eyebrows at the silly grin that spread across the younger man's face.

"If I did not know better," Mr. Phillips remarked, "I would think you in the midst of an infatuation. Has some young lady caught your eye at last?"

Thomas laughed, too pleased to be out of the house to let his attorney's assumptions bother him. "No. I am simply thrilled to be among adults. I never thought to be so glad for silence in my life. Those children have taken over my house, plain and simple, and I have no idea how to gain control again."

"They have been with you how long? A month? Surely it cannot be as bad as you say."

"If not, it is surely worse."

"Have you no governess to care for them while you carry out your business?"

Thomas sat straight up in his chair. "A governess? I had not thought of that! It is just the thing!" He looked thoughtful for a moment as hope briefly lit his face. But then he slumped back in his seat dejectedly. "Where am I to find a governess in Hertfordshire?" he bemoaned. "And quickly at that!"

Mr. Phillips took pity on the poor man. "Surely my wife would know of some suitable young lady. We are hosting a small dinner party this evening. Perhaps you might ask for suggestions there? If my wife cannot think of anyone, I have no doubt one of the other ladies present must know of someone."

Thomas frowned at the invitation. He normally avoided such social engagements as if they were a deadly disease. But desperate times called for desperate measures. He could place an ad in the papers, but that might take weeks, and he did not have the time to waste interviewing candidates.

No, one evening of discomfort was far more preferable. "I believe that would be most satisfactory."

Mr. Phillips informed him as to the details of the gathering and then they turned their attention to the business that had brought them there to begin with.

*****

Thomas checked his appearance one more time in the looking glass. His skin tingled with nerves and anticipation. He cleared his throat loudly and slid one finger under the collar that was suddenly choking him. Just as quickly, he tried to smooth his cravat back down. His valet would not be happy if he ruined all his careful work before anyone had seen it. The poor man had been thrilled at the opportunity to display his skills and dress his employer for a rare dinner party. Thomas had felt slightly guilty under the man's ministrations. His talents were sadly underutilized on him. He had almost wanted to reassure the man he would attend more social functions, just to make the poor chap feel his efforts were appreciated.

But he had stopped the words just in time, as he remembered the last fiasco of a ball that he had attended. He shuddered to think of his stammering replies and stilted dances. He had regaled one young lady with the entire history of the quadrille during their set, only to overhear her later making fun of him to her friend.

It had not been an enjoyable night. His only consolation was that he had not been the only one who had made a fool of himself at the Netherfield ball. It had seemed the whole of the Bennet family had subjected themselves to ridicule. Even their cousin, Mr. Collins, had made a complete idiot of himself, speaking so presumptuously to the illustrious Mr. Darcy, when he had not even been introduced to the man!

That had been almost four years ago now, and he had rarely ventured into society since.

He had tried to prepare himself for the evening to come, but already any confidence he might have possessed had dwindled into awkwardness. He sighed. Best be on with it. Waiting only made the task seem that much more formidable.

He descended the stairs to the waiting carriage below.

*****

Mrs. Phillips had been horrified by her husband's announcement that he had invited Mr. Bowen to their dinner party. "Why on earth would you invite *that man* to our home?! He can hardly be considered agreeable, and he is certainly not handsome! Even though he *does* have five thousand a year, all he does is drabble on about nothing at all!"

Mr. Phillips chuckled at his wife's effusions. "*That man*, as you so eloquently put it, is in desperate need of some female advice. I believed that you, with your extensive knowledge of the society in these parts, could be of assistance. Was I wrong to assume so?"

Mrs. Phillips puffed up at his words. "No! No! You are quite right. If there is anything to be known I shall know it. There is nothing that passes that escapes my notice. All of Meryton is aware that!"

"Then I was quite right to invite him to dine with us. You shall be of the utmost assistance to him."

"Of course I shall be!" she huffed. "He would not find better information in all of Hertfordshire!"

*****

Mrs. Phillips had put forth special effort to make Thomas feel welcome upon his arrival. She was pleased to have her opinion sought, and the compliment to her vanity far outweighed her prejudice against the man.

There was no time for private conversation before they all went in to dinner, so Thomas had to content himself with biding his time until tea was served. It was a difficult thing to do, given his dislike for social engagements in general, but he sought to make himself agreeable by conversing with Miss Long, who was seated to his right.

"Did you know, Miss Long, that the word dinner, as we know it now, is derived originally from the Latin word *disjējūnāre,* which meant to break one's fast? Of course, that is also where we derive the word breakfast. Not from *disjējūnāre,* I mean, but from breaking one's fast. I think breakfast is a decidedly boring word, do you not agree? It means exactly what it sounds like. There is no enjoyment in the discovery at all."

Miss Long looked up from where she had been prodding her peas about her plate. "I had no idea you were so, er… *knowledgeable…* on the matter, Mr. Bowen."

Thomas warmed to his subject. "Oh, yes. I find linguistics and etymology to be quite fascinating. The word etymology is itself quite diverting. It originates from two Greek words: *étymo,* meaning true, and *logos,* meaning word or reason. So, when put together, they mean true word or true reason. You see, then, how that clarifies the word, since you are looking for the true reason of the word, not a false or an assumed basis. Etymology therefore requires quite diligent study if you are to uncover the complete meaning and history of the word, because all one's assumptions must be pushed aside and the truth only must be carefully sought."

Thomas concluded his monologue enthusiastically, as it was one of his favorite subjects, only to come to the realization that Miss Long's eyes had long since glazed over, and although she was diligently nodding along to everything he said, her attention had drifted. Almost as soon as he had stopped speaking, she turned decidedly to her other dinner companion, engaging him with some town gossip she had overheard.

Thomas turned his attention to the lady on his left, hoping to converse with her, only to be met with the back of her head, as she was firmly engaged in speaking to the gentleman on her other side.

His cheeks flushed with two bright spots of pink as he came to the conclusion that both young ladies were pointedly avoiding talking to him. He lowered his head and applied himself to his meal in an effort to cover his embarrassment. He had done it again, despite his best intentions.

He should have known better than to bring up etymology. He had simply been trying to find a common ground to converse about. Surely, any accomplished young lady, as those around him claimed to be, would have been interested in acquiring knowledge. But, if the conversations around him held any evidence, the young ladies were more interested in acquiring and spreading the village gossip than pursuing knowledge.

He sighed and fiddled with his roast beef. He would never learn how to fit in with polite society.

After that debacle, dinner was just something to be endured and got through as quickly as possible. There could be no real enjoyment in the meal. Thomas felt some relief when the ladies adjourned to the parlor, leaving the gentlemen to their port. But even here, he was afraid to open his mouth, lest he should commit some further social gaffe, especially as the conversation drifted into topics he would prefer to leave untouched.

He shifted uncomfortably as the alcohol flowed liberally, loosening too many tongues. He sat stiffly through the men's ribald jokes and knowing winks, coughing at the cloud of cigar smoke that fogged the room.

When they were finally able to rejoin the ladies in the parlor, Thomas had developed a pounding headache and had no desire to do anything but obtain the information he needed and politely excuse himself. Even the noise at home was preferable to this.

To his delight, he was able to accomplish his objective with very little effort on his part. Mrs. Phillips, once tea had been served, sought him out.

"I have been informed, Mr. Bowen, that you have need of a lady's opinion," she said proudly, batting her eyes and preening. "How may I be of service?"

Thomas, while repulsed by her vain display, was not about to let the opportunity pass him by. He cleared his throat and wiped his sweaty palms on his pants. "Yes. Well. About a month ago, as you are probably aware, my sister died, and her husband being at sea, I, umm, *inherited* her children. I have found that I have no affinity for the children, and your husband suggested to me, just this morning, that I should acquire a governess. I at once agreed, but I have not the slightest idea where to obtain one on such short notice.

I was hoping you might know of some suitable young lady in the neighborhood. Just someone to come during the day and see to them."

Mrs. Phillips leaned back in her chair to ponder this perplexity. She tapped one long finger against her lips and tried to put on a brooding air. Immediately, a young lady sprang to mind, but she pretended to think a little longer, to make it seem like she had really given the matter serious thought.

"One of my nieces, Miss Mary Bennet, is said to be the most accomplished young lady in the neighborhood. She is not perhaps as beautiful or as gregarious as some of the other young ladies, but I believe she should suit your purposes exactly. You will find her most amiable and I believe she would appreciate an excuse to get out of the house."

Thomas thanked Mrs. Phillips for her valuable assistance and took his leave. As his carriage pulled away from the entry, he turned his mind to Miss Mary Bennet. He knew very little about the young lady in question.

He remembered briefly passing through the room as she played the pianoforte at the Netherfield Ball. Her choice of music had perhaps been a little off for the venue, but he remembered being impressed with her level of skill at the instrument. Other than that, he only had a vague impression of a quiet brunette, overshadowed by her more vivacious sisters.

But it was a start. For the first time, he felt hope that he could stop the downward spiral that had begun when his sister's children had first stepped foot into his home. He thought wistfully of a return to his structured lifestyle and harmony within the four walls of his home.

If Mary Bennet could give him that, he would be eternally grateful to her.

Other books by Lelia M. Silver

The story of Pride and Prejudice continues with…
The Children of Pride and Prejudice series

Emilia's Folly

John's Downfall

Sophia's Champion

Thea's Legacy

Helene's Honor

Hannah's Viscount

Theo's Choice

Eliza's Journey

Pride and Prejudice goes for a spin in the Old West with…

Pemberley Creek series

Pride and Presumption

Pride and Perfection

A modern twist to Pride and Prejudice

Pride and Precipice